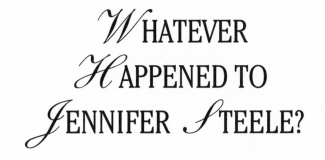

Whatever Happened to Jennifer Steele?

ALSO BY JEAN RURYK

Chicken Little Was Right

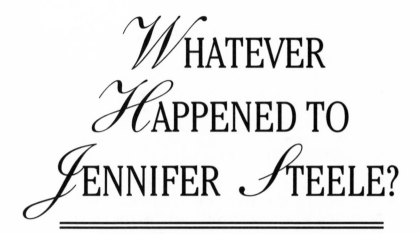

WHATEVER HAPPENED TO JENNIFER STEELE?

A CAT WILDE MYSTERY

JEAN RURYK

ST. MARTIN'S PRESS

NEW YORK

For France_____ with appreciation.

A THOMAS DUNNE BOOK.
An imprint of St. Martin's Press.

WHATEVER HAPPENED TO JENNIFER STEELE? Copyright © 1996 by Jean Ruryk. All rights reserved. Printed in the United States of America. No part of this book may be used or reproduced in any manner whatsoever without written permission except in the case of brief quotations embodied in critical articles or reviews. For information, address St. Martin's Press, 175 Fifth Avenue, New York, N.Y. 10010.

Design by Basha Zapatka

Library of Congress Cataloging-in-Publication Data

Ruryk, Jean.
    Whatever happened to Jennifer Steele? : a Cat Wilde mystery / by Jean Ruryk.—1st ed.
       p.   cm.
    "A Thomas Dunne book."
    ISBN 0-312-14067-3
    I. Title.
    PR9199.3.R79W48   1996
    813'.54—dc20   95-40806
                                            CIP

First Edition: March 1996

10 9 8 7 6 5 4 3 2 1

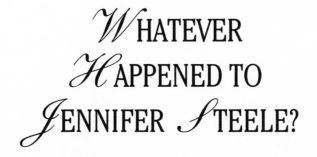

WHATEVER HAPPENED TO JENNIFER STEELE?

1

She's back." Charlie gestured with his bearded chin. "And it's your turn."

Rafe grimaced. "No way. I just had lunch."

I turned to look. Other than the three of us, and a shop full of artfully displayed overpriced antiques, the place was empty.

"Call Larry," Rafe said irritably. "Let him handle her."

"Handle who?" I was surprised by his uncharacteristic testiness. "Nobody here but us chickens."

"In the window. The bag lady," Charlie growled. "She's been hanging around out there for two days. We give her a couple of bucks and she goes away for a while." He flung an exasperated arm in the air, bellowing, "Larry! Get out here!"

"He's out back loading my car." I held out my hand. "Give me the money. I'll do it."

"You'll be sorry, Cat," Rafe warned.

"Why?" I looked from Rafe to Charlie.

"Well." He shrugged. "She's maybe a little bit ripe."

"A little bit ripe?" Rafe snorted. "She smells like a soggy crotch."

"Crudely put." Charlie's nose wrinkled. "Also true." He handed me two dollar bills. "Here. Don't inhale."

She stood in the recessed shop door alcove, her gaze intent on the display inside. Her right hand rested on the handle of a wire basket cart stuffed with crumpled plastic bags.

She turned her head as I unlatched the door and I was startled to see that this was no old crone. This bag lady was a young woman, pale-faced, with one inflamed eye glaring out from under a dingy beret pulled low over the other. Then I was thrown back as she lunged through the opening doorway.

While I staggered for balance she snatched a vase from the display window.

It hit with my first intake of breath. Sour, stale body odor and an acrid stench of urine.

"It's mine." She pressed the vase closer, hunching her shoulders protectively. "It's mine."

Her voice was light with a raw edge of huskiness. It was a voice I knew well.

"I'm not stealing it." She delved into the pocket of her ragged sweater and produced some crumpled bills. "I'll pay for it."

There was no mistaking that voice. "Jen?" I peered at her, disbelieving my ears. "Jenny?"

To my astonishment, she dropped. One moment we were face-to-face, the next she was a crumpled heap at my feet.

Charlie and Rafe gaped, as dumbfounded as I was.

"What the hell?" Charlie bustled from the rear of the shop. He bent and snatched the vase, a black art deco piece. "Jesus, Cat. What did you say to her?"

"Forget what Cat said." Rafe joined us. He snapped at Charlie, "Just get her out of here."

"Sure," Charlie snarled back. "What do you want me to do? Roll her back out on the street?"

Rafe gestured silently toward the shop entrance. A man with silver hair hesitated outside the door, frowned, made up his mind, and hurried away.

"Shit." Charlie handed Rafe the vase, bent, and gathered the woman into his arms. "Cat? Bring her cart, will you?"

He headed for the rear of the shop, carrying her as easily as he would a child. I wheeled her cart in from the street and followed Rafe to the storage room, wondering if I had imagined that voice.

Charlie had dropped her onto a wicker chaise, the only nonupholstered piece of furniture in the room.

I didn't blame him.

The jeans she wore were threadbare and dirty. Her bare toes poked through ragged holes in her dingy white sneakers.

The knit cardigan may once have been blue. It was now an undefinable shade, heavily stained.

Her face was waxen, translucent skin stretched tightly over sharply defined bones. Her lips were the color of clay. Sooty smudges undershadowed each eye. An angry sty distorted one eyelid.

But it was Jenny's face.

I pulled off the gray beret. The matted, unwashed hair was the right color. Strawberry blond.

Her eyes opened abruptly. Cornflower blue, with no trace of recognition in their depths. Her gaze wavered past me to where Rafe had entered and now stood, the vase in one hand, her money in the other.

She shifted, let her feet fall to the floor. With effort she pushed herself upright and stood, her calves braced against the chaise. Her sweatered arms hung like empty tubes.

"It's mine," she said. She cleared her throat, attempted a more aggressive tone. "It's mine. But I'll pay for it."

The two-note *bing-bong* of the shop doorbell chimed softly and remotely. Charlie, an expression of relief on his face, shot his cuffs.

"Saved by the bell," he muttered. Brushing fussily at his jacket sleeves, he escaped into the store.

"I'll pay you," she repeated. The momentary forcefulness had fled. Her voice was an echo in an empty room. The blue eyes had dulled.

"Sure you will." Rafe waved the crumpled bills. "With our own money? Forget it."

She blinked. Her eyes darted around the room, bounced off my face, and lit on the vase. Her lips thinned in a way I remembered.

"Give it to her, Rafe," I said. "I'll pay for it."

Rafe's one mobile eyebrow shot up in surprise but the sharp sound of a buzzer interrupted anything he might have said. He thrust the money and the vase at me and hurried through the door to the shop.

She snatched the vase from my hand, buried it in the folds

of her sweater, and crossed her arms over her chest. We stood silently facing each other. She squinted at me and I remembered Jenny was nearsighted. I stepped closer.

"You don't know who I am, do you?" I said softly.

Her eyes closed wearily. "Lady," she said in that familiar voice, "I don't even know who *I* am."

Behind her, the tin-lined door to the alley swung wide and Larry came in, my car keys dangling from his fingers.

"All set, Cat," he said. He halted, his nose puckering. "What's that smell?"

"Larry." I waved him in. "Stay put. I'll be right back."

In the shop, Charlie was puttering aimlessly, moving a vase to the right, a figurine to the left, his eye on Rafe and a stout woman with hennaed hair and crayoned eyebrows. Their heads were together, intent on an assemblage of birds littering the counter between them. Porcelain birds, wood and glass and brass birds, large birds and small birds.

"So?" Charlie muttered as I joined him. "Did you get rid of Orphan Annie?"

I shook my head. "No. She's still there."

"What!" Charlie barked. He lowered his voice at a frown from Rafe. "You left her alone? With our stock?"

"Relax, Charlie. The only thing she's after is the vase. I came out to pay you for it. How much?"

"The vase? I don't know. Rafe priced it."

"What did you pay?"

"Hell, I don't know, Cat," Charlie said crossly. "It came in an estate sale. We paid for the job lot. Take the damn thing." His one golden eye glinted craftily. "I'll make you a deal. She takes the vase. You get rid of her."

"Deal." I nodded, then heard myself say, "I'm taking her home with me."

The words had come out unplanned, unbidden, and startled me as much as they did Charlie.

"You're *what?*" Charlie bellowed. Rafe glared. Charlie pulled me closer.

4

"Are you out of your mind, Cat?" he hissed. "Take her home? God knows what assortment of creepy crawlies she's. . . . For Christ's sake, Cat, the woman's got open sores on her wrists."

"I didn't see any sores."

"They're there. Believe me, She's probably . . ." He cut off his words abruptly. His head dipped in a courtly nod as the mahogany-haired matron sailed past us, her orange-painted lips curved in a mean smile.

Charlie waited for the shop door to close behind her.

"Was I right," he called to Rafe, "or was I right?"

"You were right." Rafe was sorting the birds, handling some with care, contemptuously dropping others into the box in which they had arrived. "The three Beswicks you spotted. Plus. A Royal Doulton flambé. A Staffordshire swan. A Lalique frosted pair. A Hutschenreuther group. A Kaiser. Two or three not bad Occupied Japan. And! One very fine, very old bronze eagle. The rest is dime-store junk."

"How much did you offer?"

Rafe raised bland eyes.

"Offer? What offer?" he said innocently. "She said she knew precisely what the collection was worth and she was not about to be taken advantage of. Was she making herself clear? I told her I understood perfectly and paid her exactly what she asked."

"And," Rafe continued, smiling broadly, "the flambé alone is worth triple what we paid for the lot. And this little beauty . . ." He picked up the bronze eagle, stroked its head, and placed it carefully on a glass shelf behind him. "So. The bag woman gone?"

"No. She is not gone." Charlie starchily enunciated each word. "Cat says she's taking her home with her. Stink, sores, and God only knows what else. Talk to her, Rafe."

Rafe eyed me thoughtfully.

"You know her, don't you?" he said.

I nodded. "Since she was twelve years old."

"When did you last see her?"

I had to stop and think. On television, when? A year? Two years? Face-to-face? "Six . . . maybe seven years ago."

"A lot happens in seven years, Cat. And street people, it's usually drugs, booze, or looney tunes."

"Not booze. She's allergic to alcohol."

"So it's not booze. So it's something else. Whatever it is, Cat, it's a problem you don't need."

"But I can't . . ." I looked from Rafe to Charlie. "What do we do? Dump her back on the street? What'll happen to her? I can't . . . there's just no way I can simply abandon her."

Rafe frowned, then shrugged, spreading his palms. "Well, I guess a woman's got to do what she's got to do," he said.

The shop doorbell ponged softly. His gaze slid past me as two women in their mid-fifties, fashionably gaunt and expensively blond, strolled into the shop. He placed the bird box out of sight under the counter.

"But if it gets sticky," he added in an undertone, "you bail out fast, okay?"

"For sure."

Charlie followed me to the rear of the shop, beaming his Sotheby's smile on the two women as we passed. He halted at the door to the storage room.

"Cat?" he said. "We'd like to know what's under the paint on those pieces you're taking. Like really soon."

"Not to worry, Charlie. I'll start on the pedestal table this afternoon," I promised.

She was seated on the wicker chaise, her knees pressed together, the vase held tightly to her breast. Her head was tilted back, her eyes closed. She had replaced the beret on her head. The dead gray color emphasized an unhealthy yellow cast in the paleness of her skin. The sty burned scarlet.

I glanced at her wrists. The sores were there, raw, red, and scabby.

Larry, legs dangling, sat across from her on a mission oak desk, studying her thoughtfully.

As I approached her eyes flew wide. Panic flashed in their depths momentarily, replaced by a wary watchfulness.

"It's all right." I reached a hand to her, then let it drop when I saw her shrink away. "It's all right, Jenny."

"You know my name?" She bent forward from the waist. The change in her was electric. Her wariness vanished. "Do you know who I am?"

"Your name is Jenny. Jenny Steele. You're Jennifer Steele."

"I knew it!" Larry pushed himself off the desk. "I knew it! Jennifer Steele! Cranberry Crush! Amanda Prentiss! Susie Squirrel!"

The eagerness in her eyes clicked off like a flicked light switch. She hunched deeper into her voluminous sweater, muttering to herself. I strained to hear. *Susiesquirrelsusie squirrelsusiesquirrel.* Susie Squirrel.

"Susie Squirrel was a puppet on a television show," I explained. "You were the voice of Susie Squirrel."

I don't know if she understood, or even heard. Her arms tightened around the vase. She began a dismal rocking back and forth, oblivious to her surroundings.

I felt a sudden sharp stab of doubt. What was I letting myself in for?

Or, more to the point, why?

Jenny Steele and my daughter Laurie became friends in their first year of high school.

At twelve Jenny was bespectacled and shy, possessed of a whiskey tenor voice, startling in a wispy body. My Laurie, tall and overweight, was a mass of nailbiting insecurities. Time and Mother Nature eventually remolded them both, but the alliance they formed in those cruel early-teen years remained steadfast until they graduated. In my memory, Laurie's high school years were inextricably bound with Jenny's.

Which was fine. Until now.

Because, now, Laurie is dead.

And because, from now on, whenever I remember her as a girl, my mind will fast-forward and present me with this sour-smelling bag lady. I can walk away, but this stinking creature is going to live side by side with Laurie forever.

I turned away from her and found Larry was watching me, an oddly intent expression on his face.

"Would you mind putting Jenny's cart in my car for me?" I asked. "Please?"

He nodded, with what seemed to me more approval than assent. "Sure, Cat." He wheeled the cart to the alley door.

Jenny caught movement out of the corner of her eye. Her body twisted, following Larry. "Hey." Her voice was hollow, without conviction. "Hey," she repeated.

"It's okay, Jenny. He's just putting it in my car."

Her head swivelled. She regarded me with lackluster eyes. Her eyelids drooped, a slow and weary blink.

"Who're you?" she asked tonelessly.

"Catherine Wilde. I'm taking you home with me. It's all right, Jenny. I'm a friend. A friend of yours."

I put my hand on her shoulder to reassure her, felt her stiffen. I let my hand drop.

"Let's go home," I said.

For a moment there was no reaction from her. Then, as though the words, passing through defective wiring, had touched off a spark in her brain's command center, she moved. Pushing herself up from the chaise, she shuffled after me to the lane where Larry waited beside my car.

With a gentle flourish he helped her into the passenger seat. She melted back, her eyes closed, her arms wrapped around the vase, oblivious to his straining past her to reach the seat belt buckle.

After a moment of awkward indecision, he arranged the belt across her arms and clicked the buckle into its socket. He pushed the door closed and turned to me.

"Cat? I finish here at noon," he said. "I could follow you home and help unload if you like."

"It's okay." I indicated the three pieces of furniture in the rear of the station wagon. "They're not heavy."

He was too polite to press but his disappointment was obvious. I was puzzled until I saw the longing expression on his face when he glanced back at Jenny.

"Do you finish at noon tomorrow?" I asked.

He nodded absently. "I only work here in the mornings."

"Why not come for lunch tomorrow?"

His face lit up. "What time do you want me to come?"

"Whenever. Come straight from here if you like."

"I will." He beamed at me. "Thank you, Cat. Thank you."

"Hey, it's only lunch." I circled the car and got into the driver's seat. The smell inside was overpowering. I rolled the window down and leaned out. "D'you like borscht?"

"I like everything." He smiled.

He remained in the alley, dwindling in the rearview mirror, until I turned onto the street and he was gone.

Traffic was heavy. I concentrated on driving. When we were free of the downtown core, on the autoroute to the suburbs and home, I sideglanced at my silent passenger.

She was exactly as Larry had placed her. The only color in her face was the angry sty. I maneuvered into the slow lane and risked a more searching look.

There was no evident rise and fall of breath beneath the restraining seat belt. *Migod*, the thought flashed through my mind, *she's dead*.

"Jenny?" I scrambled for a natural question, found one. "When did you eat last?"

She stirred. Without opening her eyes, she said, "What day is today?"

It was said in such a normal tone of voice I briefly wondered if she was playing a part, getting into a role. She was, after all, an actress. An actress good enough to fake the eccentric behavior.

But the sty was authentic. The sores on her wrists were real. And no makeup could counterfeit the sickly pallor of her skin. The bag lady bit was no act.

I thought back to the first time I had seen her perform.

A perceptive drama teacher had recognized something in the unprepossessing teenager she had been at fourteen and cast her as the second lead in a staging of *Guys and Dolls*.

Footlights lit a spark in her, transfigured her. Her brash and brassy Miss Adelaide had brought down the house. For the balance of her high school years she was the undisputed star of every production. She had made even the dated silliness of *No, No, Nanette* palatable.

I was producing radio and television commercials at the time she graduated. A client requested a fresh face for a new product and I thought of Jenny. She became the spokesman . . . spokeswoman? Spokesperson? Whatever. She became the vocal and visual talent for Cranberry Crush.

That was the beginning.

I lined her up with an agent, a sharp, fortyish, very nice woman named Hannah Peel. Soon she had all the commercial work she could handle. She put in a season as weatherwoman on a local television station; a stretch as Miss Tiddleywinks on a kiddy show named *Kiddy Korner*.

She was doing Susie Squirrel when my life fell apart. By the time I had it together and Laurie had married and moved three hundred miles away, I had lost touch with Jenny.

She began to appear regularly on national television. A character bit on a police drama, speaking parts in several series, supporting roles in two or three television movies. I assumed she had made the move to Los Angeles. Then she turned up in a soap opera out of New York, as beautiful-but-bad Amanda Prentiss, prosecuting attorney on *Halls of Justice*.

Amanda was made to pay for her sins. She was doused with gasoline and set alight by the enemies of a crime lord with whom she was having an affair.

Adieu Amanda, exit Jenny. I hadn't seen her on-screen since Amanda's incineration.

The soap opera had been . . . a soap opera. But Jenny's portrayal of Amanda had breathed excitement into the trite script and reviewers had begun mentioning her name.

One meaty role would have done it for her, lifted her out of "cast includes" into "name above the title."

She'd been that close.

What happened? I wanted to ask the malodorous creature sitting remote and immobile beside me.

What happened to you?

2

I kvetched to myself throughout the half-hour drive home, already regretting my impulsive decision to take Jenny home with me, acknowledging at the same time that there was nothing else I could have done.

Jenny, head drooped, eyes closed, rode silently beside me, as animated as a bagful of rags.

She didn't stir when I brought the car to a halt in my driveway nor when I opened the passenger door. I released her seat belt and her eyes flew wide open, blue and empty.

"We're home," I said.

Her glance skittered past me to the house, to the lawn, to the car hood, to the vase in her arms, back to me.

"We're home," I repeated. "Come on."

She hesitated, then clambered awkwardly from the car, clutching the vase, using her elbows to push herself from the seat. This time I didn't move to help.

She shuffled several steps along the cement walk to the flagstone stoop of the house. I followed and almost walked into her when she halted abruptly. She looked back, frowning.

"We'll get your cart later," I said. *And then fumigate the car,* I thought. I took her arm. "Come on. Let's get this show on the road."

Matching my steps to her slow pace I pondered which should come first, food or a shower. My nose made the decision.

Shower first.

I laid out shampoo, fresh towels, and my terry robe, then set the water to a comfortably warm temperature. I left her in the bathroom, still hugging the damn vase, and went to the kitchen to prepare lunch.

Potato salad. Kielbasa. Slices of field-grown beefsteak tomatoes and rye bread with hard, cold butter. A tall glass of milk for her, tea for myself.

The only sound from the bathroom was the steady hiss of the shower running. No movement. No splashing. I poured a cup of tea, sat, sipped, and listened. Minutes passed and I had a sudden mental image of her, standing as I had left her, fully clothed, while the hot water tank drained.

At the moment I decided to go and pound on the door it opened. She emerged, barefoot, wrapped in the terry robe, wet hair clinging to a fragile skull. Walking slightly pigeon-toed, the way a child walks, she came down the hall, carrying her clothing and the vase. She hesitated in the doorway to the kitchen, shifting her bundle uncertainly.

"Just drop it on the floor," I said. "Come and eat."

She nodded without speaking, let the sour-smelling clothes fall to the floor, set the vase on the dishwasher, came to the table, and sat down. She clasped her hands tightly.

"I don't remember your name," she said. "I'm sorry."

"Don't be sorry. Eat. We can talk later." I picked up my fork. "My name is Catherine."

She ate too quickly. She attacked her food, barely chewing. I was momentarily repelled. Then I realized I was seeing real hunger, the hunger of a scavenging alley dog.

"Slow down," I said. "Nobody's going to take it away from you."

Her hand froze in its path to the glass of milk. She went totally still, her shoulders hunched, eyes downcast. I felt a sudden stab of exasperation, directed partly at her, mostly toward myself.

"Forget it. Forget it." I flapped an irritated hand. "Go ahead. Eat."

Warily, without lifting her eyes, she picked up the milk. As she drank, draining the glass without pause, her sleeve fell back exposing pale, blue-veined skin. Raw sores and scabs extended up her inner arm to the bend of her elbow. My scalp prickled. I'd heard of drug needle tracks but never seen them. Was this how they looked?

I pushed away from the table, went to the fridge for more milk. The potato salad was beside the milk carton and I glanced back to see if she had cleaned her plate.

She was slumped in her chair, elbows on the table, her hands splayed out. I shut the fridge door.

When I touched her shoulder I felt her body leap under my fingers as though she'd been stung. Her head reared back. Her unfocused glance bounced about the room then fixed on me. There was no sign of recognition in her eyes.

"Come on," I said. "If you're going to snooze you may as well do it in bed."

I returned to the kitchen and sat brooding over a cup of tepid tea. I had seen the scabs behind her ears, exposed by the slicked-back hair, the sores on her bare ankles and on the tender skin behind her knees.

Forget needle tracks. What does AIDS look like?

I dumped the cold tea in the sink, went to the phone, and dialed Dan Freedman's number. Three rings and a breezy voice chirped, "Doctor Freedman's office. May I help you?"

"Marcie? It's Catherine Wilde. Is he with a patient?"

"He's on the phone. Want me to have him call you?"

"Please."

"Death's door or merely urgent?" Marcie asked, typically abrupt. A spinal cord injury had put her in a wheelchair, ending her career as head nurse at Lakeshore General. Dan had snapped her up. Now in her mid-fifties, she runs his office with a zero tolerance for prattle. The reverse side of her desk nameplate reads LIFE'S TOO SHORT FOR BULLSHIT.

"Merely urgent," I said.

"I'll have him call you."

Ten minutes later the phone rang. It was Dan.

"You called," he stated.

"I need an appointment, Dan. As soon as you can squeeze me in. A complete physical. Blood, urine, AIDS, the whole nine yards."

"AIDS?" His gravelly voice rose an octave. "You?"

"Come on, Dan. The appointment isn't for me."

"Who's it for?"

"Jennifer Steele. I don't know if you remember her. You treated her once. Friend of Laurie's? Jenny Steele?"

"Steele. Steele." There was a momentary silence. "Skinny blond kid? Glasses? Allergic reaction to alcohol. What, ten, fifteen years ago? What's the matter with her?"

"Everything. Can you see her?"

"Isn't she an actress or something now?"

"She's a bag lady or something now. Can you squeeze her in somewhere soon?"

"Can you have her at Lakeshore General at eight o'clock tomorrow morning?"

"Tomorrow?" I was startled. Two weeks was a normal lead time for an appointment with Dan.

"I was about to cancel for a patient of mine. Just hung up on the widow before I called you."

"The widow? Your patient died?"

"Oh, he died all right, the silly son of a bitch." Dan snorted angrily. "Quit smoking I tell him, it's going to kill you. Go on a diet, lose fifty pounds. All that lard's going to kill you. Cut down on the booze, I tell him. Christ."

"What happened? Heart attack?"

"Hell, no. I forgot to warn him about screwing around." Exasperation replaced the anger in his voice. "The damn fool was *shtupping* his top salesman's wife. So the salesman comes home in the middle of the afternoon and finds them making waves on the water bed. Gets a gun and shoots holes in all three of them. Boss, wife, and water bed. So then he goes and drinks himself *non compos mentis* until the police arrive at one in the morning because the soggy plaster ceiling in the apartment below collapses and damn near kills an old couple in their bed. Christ."

I had to choke back an impulse to laugh. "Dan," I said, "you're making this up."

"Aw hell, Catherine," he said wearily. "I wish I was. I liked the silly bastard. I like his wife. I like his kids. I like his two-year-old granddaughter. So now all these nice people are going to be media fodder because that *meshugge* son of a bitch couldn't keep his pecker in his pants."

His heavy sigh sang across the wires. Then, suddenly brusque, he said, "Have her at Lakeshore at eight, okay? No food, nothing to drink after midnight. And don't forget the urine sample."

He hung up.

Lifting the tailgate of my car released the unpleasant smell emanating from her cart. I wheeled it around the house to the rear patio and went back for Rafe's furniture.

There were three pieces. A small sewing cabinet, a plant stand with three shelves, and a tilt-top candle stand, each painted a muddy shade of olive green, ombréd with sepia and flecked in darker brown.

"Antiquing," Rafe had said disgustedly. "Twenty, twenty-five years ago, this idiotic fad for antiqueing. Slather on some paint, smear some burnt umber, spatter dots around with a toothbrush. Presto! Antique. I cringe when I think how much good furniture must have been violated by a bunch of amateurs being—God help us—creative."

"Well, at least whoever did these didn't beat them with chains and drill wormholes." Charlie patted the sewing cabinet. "Rafe thinks this is Gallé," he said to me.

"Gallé? Emile Gallé? Porcelain and glass Emile Gallé? I didn't know Gallé did furniture."

"Late eighteen hundreds. Gorgeous stuff." Rafe's brows lifted. "You've never seen pictures of the Gallé bed?"

"Never. What makes you think this is a Gallé?"

"The cow parsley motif." Rafe traced the leaves carved into the sides of the cabinet. "Gallé liked cow parsley. This piece probably has a marquetry top. If we're lucky there'll be a signature. Possibly inlaid. He worked in fairly soft woods, so go gently, Cat."

I decided to do the sewing cabinet first.

On the rear patio I laid out stripper and 000 steel wool—if

it was soft wood with inlay I couldn't use a spatula—plus rags, newspapers, a garbage bin, and heavy rubber gloves. I went into the house, put Leona Boyd on the CD, changed to paint-stained T-shirt and jeans and got to work.

Twenty minutes later I steel-wooled away the last of the paint and stripper guck from the top of the cabinet and there it was, integrated into an inlaid pattern of vine leaves. The signature Rafe hoped for. Two words in a flowing art nouveau script: *Gallé. Nancy.*

I shucked the rubber gloves and scurried to the kitchen phone.

"Canterbury House Antiques. Charles Harwood here. May I help you?" He spoke in the lofty British tones Rafe claimed made him sound as though he'd been impaled on a Buckingham Palace flagpole.

"Climb down, Charlie. It's only me. Rafe was right. It's Gallé. Inlaid signature. Gallé. Nancy."

The accent vanished. "Hey, Cat! Great! Hold on."

I heard him call out. "Rafe! It's Cat. You were right. It's Gallé." I could hear Rafe's voice but couldn't make out his words. Then Charlie was back. "Rafe wants to know about the plant stand."

"Haven't touched it yet. All I've done is the top of the sewing cabinet."

"Leave the cabinet for the meanwhile, Cat. We know what it is. Go at the plant stand. And call as soon as you find anything. Okay?"

"Sure."

It took two hours to strip the stand, shelf by shelf. Most of the time and effort went into the intricate carving on the tall slender legs. The piece was graceful, beautiful. But no marquetry. No signature. I went back to the phone.

This time Rafe answered. "This is Canterbury House. May I help you?"

"The plant stand? Sorry, Rafe. No marquetry. Just plain mahogany. But very interesting legs. All that floral carving? Not wood. Metal. I'd guess bronze."

"Bronze?" There was excitement in Rafe's voice. "What are the flowers? I mean, can you tell what kind of flowers?"

"They look like water lilies to me. Flowers floating on round leaf pads. I'd say water lilies."

"Majorelle! It has to be Majorelle."

"Who's Majorelle?"

"Louis Majorelle. A Frenchman. Influenced by Gallé. Cat? When do you think they'll be ready?"

"All three?"

"Forget the candle stand for the moment. It's probably maple, early American. Concentrate on the two French pieces. When can we have them?"

"The two? Friday. It'll have to be Friday. I have a table from Irving I've promised for Monday. I can do that over the weekend. How's Friday?"

"Irving Getz? Why're you doing work for Irving?"

"His money's the same color as yours, Rafe."

"Huh." Rafe grunted. "Watch yourself with him, Cat. Get your money on delivery and don't take his check. We've been hearing rumors."

"What kind of rumors?"

"Hasn't paid off on some consignment items. Defaulted on an auction bid. Those kind of rumors. Plus I heard he's being sued for misrepresenting a painting. It's been a couple of tough years lately and I think he's skating pretty close to the edge, so watch it."

"Thanks, Rafe. I will."

The sun had dipped behind the cedar hedges, a dark cloud overhead was beginning to spit rain, and I was feeling the first pangs of hunger by the time the Gallé was finished. I carried the three pieces into the house, left them in the living room, and went back to clean up the mess on the patio.

Back in the kitchen I was tempted to cram the clothes she had worn into the garbage along with the gummy rags and crumpled newspapers. Instead I carried them out to the patio and heaped them on top of the bags in her cart.

A faintly sour smell lingered in the kitchen. I switched on the ceiling fan. I opened a jar of spaghetti sauce, put a pot of water on to boil, then went for a quick shower and a change of clothing.

On the way back to the kitchen I glanced into the spare bedroom. She lay facing away, curled in the fetal position, so still that I waited until the barely perceptible rise and fall of the blanket assured me she was alive.

While I set the pasta on to boil and put together a salad I debated letting her sleep. If she slept through the night, with no breakfast permitted, she wouldn't eat again till noon tomorrow. And if lunch today was any indication, she needed food a lot more than she needed sleep.

As I circled the bed to waken her, she moaned, a deep wrenching sound. Her face contorted into a grimace of horror. Behind closed lids her eyes rolled like loose marbles. She shuddered, her clawed hand scrabbling at the blanket.

The spasm passed as quickly as it had come. Her face melted into serenity, her straining fingers slackened and curled into a sleeping child's fist.

"Jenny." I touched her shoulder with a wary hand. "Wake up. Supper's ready. Jenny?"

She surprised me.

I had expected another of her wide-lidded, startled awakenings. Instead, her eyes opened gently, almost dreamily. She raised up and braced herself against the headboard, clutching the terry robe to her throat.

"Where am I?" she said.

"You're in my house. You're in Laurie's room. Do you remember Laurie?"

She shook her head.

"Do you remember me? Catherine?"

Her frown deepened. Behind her eyes I could see wheels begin to turn. "Catherine." She nodded. "Catherine?" Anxiety flickered in her expression. "My vase? Where's my vase?"

"In the kitchen. Right where you left it. Come on. Supper's ready."

This time she ate without haste, twirling strands of spaghetti on her fork as I outlined the morning ahead.

"We have to be there at eight. No breakfast. We'll need a urine sample. They'll be checking you from top to bottom. A complete physical. Do you understand what I'm saying?"

She looked up from her salad. The fiery sty distorted her eyelid but her eyes were clear and blue. She nodded. Squinting past me to the dishwasher where the vase stood, she frowned.

"My clothes . . ." she began hesitantly. "My clothes?"

"They're on the patio. With your cart." I shook my head. "You can't wear them tomorrow. We'll dig up something of mine for you. Jeans, a dress, whatever. Probably be too big but they'll do. We're not going to a wedding."

She looked at me blankly.

"Wedding?" Suddenly her voice was wispy, an eerie echo. The abrupt change sent a chill through me. Her eyes had lost their focus. Her head drooped, too heavy for the frail column of her neck. Her shoulders melted. Her fork slipped from her fingers and dropped to the floor.

Rafe's words came back to me: booze, drugs, or looney tunes. Was a drug habit affecting the wildly fluctuating pattern of her behavior? Madness?

I waited. Perhaps there was a cycle to the strange and sudden mood swings. Two minutes on terra firma, two in the twilight zone?

Three minutes passed. Then, abruptly, she snored, a snuffling, childlike exhalation.

She was asleep.

Her body leaped when I touched her. Her head reared back, eyes flaring and frightened. I pulled her to her feet and led her back to bed. She curled into a tight ball. I turned off the light and left the room.

The rain had settled into a steady drizzle. Tidying the kitchen, I thought of wheeling her cart into the house but my nose twitched at the memory of the smell. I left it where it was and went to bed.

Okay. I rescued her from . . . whatever. I had her. What was I going to do with her?

Before I could find an answer I was asleep.

A sound.

I came fully awake, eyes and ears straining. Red digital numbers on the radio alarm flashed three-oh-seven in a room dark as pitch, silent as a stone.

The rain had ceased but no moonlight, no starshine cut the absolute blackness of the night. I waited, rigid, breath held till I heard it again, a whimpering, moaning, keening that seemed to go on forever.

Skin prickling, I slid quietly from under the sheets and groped along the wall to the bedroom door. It was open to a sharp ammonialike odor from the hallway beyond. My fingers found the light switch.

For a moment I was blinded by the sudden brilliance. I squeezed my eyes shut, opened them, and saw her, naked and trembling under the pitiless light, the floor beneath her bare feet wet with urine.

"I'm sorry. I'm sorry." Her hands fluttered to hide her nakedness. As though realizing the futility of their effort they dropped limply to her sides. Tears spilled from her pleading eyes and tracked, glistening, down her cheeks. "I couldn't . . ." Her thin body jerked in a spasm of shivering. "I c-couldn't . . . fuh . . . find the bathroom."

The resentment and distaste I had felt for the grungy bag lady dissolved in a rush of pity for Jenny.

"It's all right. It's all right." I reached into the hall closet for a bath towel. "Here. Stand on this. It's my fault. I should have left a night-light for you. Stay put a minute. I'll get you a nightgown. Or something."

I hurried into my room, pulled one of the oversized T-shirts I slept in from a drawer, and returned to the hall.

She hadn't moved. Her arms were crossed, covering her breasts. Spots of color bloomed on her pale cheeks but the trembling had stopped. She raised her arms when I held up the shirt and I slipped it over her head. I led her back to bed and stayed with her, stroking her hair until she slept.

I threw the soggy towel into the bath tub and crawled back to my own bed wondering if she could manufacture enough urine for the morning sample.

Well, what the hell. We could wring out the towel.

3

I don't suppose you remember Dr. Freedman?" I glanced at her in the passenger seat beside me.

She had awakened on planet earth. I'd let her sleep till the last possible moment then rushed her from bedroom to bathroom to car.

She was dressed in a blue cotton shirt. Jeans, too large, secured by a rope belt. And sneakers, two sizes too large, laced tightly. In a bottle in a bag on her lap was the required urine sample.

She shook her head. "No."

"He treated you once. You and Laurie were thirteen."

The traffic light clicked to green. I pressed down on the accelerator and inched into the solid wall of traffic on Lakeshore Boulevard.

"It was New Year's Eve. You were staying with us for the holidays that year. Anyway, it was New Year's Eve and I was at the Freedman's. Their apartment was two down from ours. A few minutes after midnight Laurie came screaming down the hall. You were choking, you were dying, you were dead."

I smiled to myself at the memory. Laurie, at thirteen, dealt only in superlatives.

"The two of you decided to do a little celebrating of your own. Champagne, if I remember correctly. Your face puffed up like a balloon and you were having trouble breathing. We rushed you to the hospital, Dan and I. They pumped out your stomach and we brought you home."

I shot a look at her. Her head had slumped, her chin on her chest. Her eyes were closed.

"And that's how we learned you're allergic to alcohol." I finished the story to myself.

Dan had arrived before us.

He looked at Jenny, noted her remoteness, sent her off to be weighed and measured, and ushered me into a small office behind the nurse's station.

"Okay." He perched on the corner of the desk. "Tell me everything you know about her."

He listened, nodding occasionally. When I finished he glanced at his watch.

"Okay. Go shopping or something. Be back nine-thirtyish. No. Make it ten. We should have some answers by then."

I went for breakfast first, then dawdled through a local hardware store, picking up steel wool, stain and varnish and sandpaper—the tools of my trade. I restore furniture for a living, mainly antiques for dealers.

I was back before ten.

Dan arrived promptly at ten, a file folder in his hand. He put his arm around my shoulders and led me into the office we'd occupied earlier.

"Siddown," he ordered. He circled the desk, seated himself, opened the folder, and spread out the papers. "Test results," he said. "And no, Catherine, she don't got AIDS."

"Results? Already?"

Dan grinned. He's a bear of a man, built, as he says, like a brick shithouse. His salt-and-pepper mane of hair and scraggly beard are trimmed, since Sylvia died, only when Marcie threatens to quit unless he visits a barber. His eyes send out wicked flashes of hazel when he smiles.

"One of Marcie's old buddies is head of the lab. I ask, I get." He sobered and tapped a sheet of blue paper clipped to an X-ray negative. "Let's start at the top. Her head."

He separated the paper from the negative.

"I'll keep it simple," he said. "You can study the X ray later if you like. The bottom line is this. She's suffered trauma to her head. Twice. A year ago, give or take a couple of months. One of the two was properly treated, eighteen stitches. The other was not."

"Could that account for her loss of memory?"

"Wait." He pushed the blue paper aside.

"She's malnourished," he continued. "Underweight. She's anemic. Folic acid deficiency. She has cystitis . . ."

"What's cystitis?"

"Bladder inflammation. Cystitis. And she has scabies."

"Scabies?"

"The sores." He closed the folder. "That about covers it. Anything you want to ask before I start?"

I leaned forward. "Dan? Any signs of drug abuse?"

His brows lifted. "Drugs? Is that what you thought?"

"Well . . . the odd behavior."

He shook his head. "Nope. No indication she abused, or has ever abused, drugs. The behavior is a symptom of folic acid deficiency. Confusion, some memory loss. Fatigue."

"One minute she's there," I interjected. "Lucid, more or less. The next she's not. Does the folic acid deficiency account for that?"

"Not entirely. Some. Plus the injuries to her head. Think of two live wires blowing in the wind. They'll touch and a connection is made. Then a gust'll blow them apart and she's off in the wild blue yonder again."

"The falling asleep? Her head sags and she's gone. I wondered about narcolepsy."

"No," he said. "Anemia. Serious malnourishment. Fitful sleep opportunities, if she's been on the street. She has no resources, no stamina. Fatigue hits her and she drops, that's it, that's all."

"She doesn't know who she is, Dan. She doesn't remember Laurie. Nor me. Is that the anemia?"

"No." He frowned. "I believe the major memory loss is a result of the head trauma. You don't know if she's been in a car accident or anything like that?"

"I don't know anything, Dan. I don't know where she's been or what's happened to her. What you see is what we get."

"Okay." He reached into his pocket, withdrew a pad and pen. "We've given her a jolt of B-12. You'll pick up folic acid tablets and see that she takes them. The tablets and a diet.

Liver. Oranges. Salads. Every green vegetable you can think of and lots of them. All those good vitamin things should take care of the behavior. Plus getting all the sleep she needs, she should be making sense in a couple of days."

"The memory loss?"

He grimaced. "I don't know about that. We'll have to wait and see." He tore a page off the pad, began another. "Antibiotics for the cystitis. This'll clear that up, no problem." He ripped off the second page. "Salve for the scabies. And some instructions."

He handed the three prescriptions to me.

"Scabies is caused by a mite that lays eggs under the skin. It's the scratching that causes the sores. The mites spread fast but they don't live long away from the body. So I want you to put fresh sheets on her bed every day until the condition clears. Fresh clothing every day. And don't you use any towels she's used."

I nodded.

"I'll want to see her again. Call me Monday."

I nodded again. "Where is she now?"

"They're working on the sty." He checked his watch. "She should be back any second." He looked up at me. "A couple of things, Catherine. She's lucky you found her now. A month, maybe two, and . . ." His shoulders lifted, fell. "You done good, kid."

I smiled at him. "That's one thing. What's the other?"

"Try to find out about the vase. In her condition, it would take an almost superhuman effort to fixate on any one idea for longer than a minute or two. You say she came back to the shop a couple of days running?"

"That's what Charlie and Rafe say."

"Then I'd say the vase has to be important to her, one way or another. Maybe if you can find out why you might be able to trigger her memory."

"I'll try."

"Don't press her," he warned. "Her memory may return in fits and starts. If she asks a question, answer the question.

Period. Too much information will blow her circuits. Do you understand what I'm saying?"

"Of course. It's the same advice you gave me when Laurie started asking questions about sex."

"Exactly."

4

We went shopping.

I had considered taking her for an eye test and glasses but Dan had vetoed the idea.

"You can remove the dressing tonight. Bathe the eye in boracic for a day or two, then go for the glasses."

We bought shoes, jeans, underwear, and T-shirts, had the three prescriptions filled, and were on our way home by twelve-thirty, later than I had expected.

A small silvery-gray car was in my driveway. Larry waited on the doorstep, a long French loaf in one hand, a white pastry box tied with blue string dangling from his fingers.

"I brought a baguette for the borscht," he called as I turned off the motor, "and a peach flan for dessert."

The words were directed at me but his eyes were on Jenny. He brightened when she stepped from the car.

The contrasting whiteness of the gauze bandage taped over her eye made her face seem less pallid. She had dozed through the drive home and her shuffling gait was replaced, momentarily at least, with a surer step.

And she was clean.

"Hey." Larry thrust the bread and pastry box into my hands. He hurried to her and reached out for the shopping bags she carried. "Looking good, Jennifer."

Her fists tightened on the plastic handles. One wide blue eye fastened on me and I guessed she had no memory of Larry. He was a stranger and a threat.

"Larry's a friend, Jen," I assured her. "You met him yesterday. He's having lunch with us."

She relinquished the bags. Larry, looking nonplused, followed us into the house.

Ten minutes later, his spirits restored, he spooned sour cream into his borscht and smiled across the table at Jenny.

"I've seen everything you've ever done," he announced.

Jenny looked up, startled, glanced at me, returned her attention to her plate. She ate slowly, methodically.

"You were the Cranberry Crush lady, remember? That was first." Larry stirred his soup until the deep red of the beet soup turned a creamy pink. "I was thirteen years old. I called the television station and got a schedule of when the commercial would appear. I saw it every single time it played, can you believe it?"

Larry looked down at his plate. He was stirring without purpose now.

"When I was thirteen I pretended you were my sister. When I was sixteen I pretended I was you." He leaned forward, presenting a smiling face to Jenny. "Don't you think we look alike?"

He was right. There was a resemblance. Both were blue-eyed, both blond. More, their bone structure was the same, fragile and somehow close to the surface. They could easily be taken for brother and sister.

Jenny's one eye inspected him. "You're prettier," she said.

Her spoon clattered to the table.

I pushed my chair back, reached her as her head tilted.

"Come on, Jenny." I slipped my hand under her arm. "It's been a long morning. Why don't you lie down for a bit."

She rose unsteadily and I led her, shuffling again, to her bedroom, covered her with a blanket, and closed the door quietly behind me.

Larry waited in the kitchen doorway, his face a mixture of anxiety and bewilderment.

"Was it something I said?" he asked.

"What?"

"I mean, that's the story of my life." He grimaced unhappily. "I open my mouth and something stupid comes out."

"Oh, Larry. No." I patted his shoulder. "It had nothing to do with you. I'll explain while we finish lunch."

He listened intently while I told him everything Dan had told me.

"She really doesn't know who she is?" he said when I finished. "She doesn't know she's Jennifer Steele?"

"She not only doesn't know who she is, she doesn't know who Jennifer Steele is."

"Will she ever remember?"

"Will she get her memory back? I don't know. Dan doesn't know. We'll have to wait and see."

Larry frowned thoughtfully. I picked up our soup bowls and carried them to the sink, plugged in the kettle for tea, and cut wedges of peach flan for the two of us. Larry watched in preoccupied silence until I sat down again.

"Cat," he said. "I can help."

"Help? How?"

"I have tapes of everything she's ever done." He pushed aside the flan and gestured eagerly, spreading his hands wide. "I taped everything. Commercials. Everything. I've got fourteen hours of *Halls of Justice* on tape."

I stared at him, dumbfounded.

"Suppose I came every day. I'd bring my own lunch," he added hastily. "Suppose I showed her the tapes. Maybe seeing herself? Maybe it would help her remember? Don't you think it might work?"

"It's worth a try." I nodded agreement. "When do you want to start?"

"Tomorrow?" His face was alight. "I could start tomorrow, if that's all right with you?"

It was fine with me. He left, elated.

Putting the sour cream and the flan into the fridge, I checked supplies. No liver. And other than a head of romaine lettuce, no green vegetables. No oranges. None of those good vitamin things.

Shopping first. Then finish stripping the Gallé table.

Fourteen hours of *Halls of Justice?* Migod.

Gallé may have liked cow parsley. I didn't. It took three hours to get the ugly green paint out of the curlicues and crevices

without damaging the soft wood. I had hoped to strip the candle stand as well but the setting sun had dipped behind the
cedars, leaving the patio in dusky twilight.

Tomorrow.

Jenny woke serenely.

"Supper in about fifteen minutes," I told her. "If you get
up now we can take care of your eye before we eat."

While I cooked—boiled potatoes with chopped green onions and sour cream, green beans, dark green spinach salad
with green peppers, liver cut in strips and sautéed with green
broccoli—she sat at the kitchen table, bathing her eye with a
boracic powder solution.

The sty had been lanced, leaving her eyelid reddened but
more or less back to a normal shape.

"Catherine?" She turned one eye on me, the other hidden
behind a wet cotton ball. "What day is it?"

"Day?" She'd remembered my name. Things were improv-
ing. "It's Wednesday. Wednesday, September eighteenth."

"September?" She dropped the cotton into the boracic and
stared at me with both wide blue eyes. "It was July the last
time I noticed. Didn't we have August this year?"

"We did." I carried her plate to the table, removed the
bowl of boracic. "Cold and rainy. You didn't miss a thing."

I brought my own plate and sat across from her. As we ate I
told her of the test results, of Dan's prognosis. She listened,
eating hungrily. But slowly.

She was thoughtful when I finished, then threw me a question out of left field.

"How old am I?"

"You're twenty-nine, Jenny. You'll be thirty in May," I replied. And felt the familiar throb of sorrow. Laurie would
have been thirty in June.

"Is that all?" She looked at me with helpless weariness.
"Twenty-nine going on ninety-two is how I feel."

I stood up hastily.

"Can you hang on long enough to shower? We have to put
ointment on your sores. I have to change the sheets. You need
a fresh T-shirt to sleep in. Think you can make it?"

"If I don't, just roll me under the bed." She pushed up from her chair. "I've slept in worse places."

A sound awakened me. Moaning? A cry?

Three-fourteen, the digital clock stated.

I waited, tense, listening. The house was silent. I fell back to sleep.

5

Good morning."

I looked up from the gummy mess I was scraping.

Jenny, wrapped in my freshly laundered terry robe, stood in the screened doorway to the kitchen.

"Hi. Good morning." I yanked at my rubber gloves. "Your pills are on the kitchen table. Take them with the orange juice. I'll be right in."

The patio was a mess. Crumpled newspapers, a bowl half full of paint stripper with a limp brush floating in greenish jelly. Paste-varnish cans and rags. The Gallé, the Majorelle, and the candle stand I had been stripping.

I looked up at the sky, shimmering a blissful blue through the leaves of the massive oak tree shading the patio. Not a cloud. We were getting our August weather now and I hoped it would stay. Once the chill days and fall rains set in I would have to move indoors and work in the basement. I preferred the airy freedom of the patio. Birds and bees and butterflies for company, noxious stripper fumes wafted away on any passing breeze. I dropped the gloves on my worktable and went into the house.

Jenny was at the sink, rinsing her juice glass.

"Your eye looks better this morning." I smiled at her.

"It itches." She rubbed her lid with a fingertip.

"That means it's healing. Don't scratch. Bathe it. The blue bowl on the table is boracic." I reached for the phone and began to dial. "I have a call to make, then I'll fix us some breakfast. French toast?"

"Sounds good."

Rafe answered on the second ring. "Canterbury House. May I help you?"

"It's me, Rafe. The candle stand. It's veneer. Want me to continue? It's a repro."

"Damn. You're sure?"

"Very. The tilt-top hardware is new. The base may be maple. I haven't stripped it yet. But the top is veneer."

"Forget it then. What about the other two? When can we have them?"

"I put the first coat of varnish on this morning. The second coat'll go on this afternoon. Third tomorrow morning. I can deliver them tomorrow afternoon."

"Tomorrow? Hold on a sec."

I glanced at Jenny while I waited, phone to my ear. She dabbed her eye with a wet cotton ball, peering nearsightedly at the black vase, still on the dishwasher where she had left it two days ago.

"Cat?" Rafe was back on the line. "We're looking into an estate appraisal out your way tomorrow morning. We'll pick them up. Noonish, one o'clock. They'll be ready?"

"They'll be ready. So will lunch. If you have time."

"We'll make time. Thanks, Cat." He hung up.

Gathering ingredients for French toast, I asked Jenny about the vase.

"Dan thinks if you remember why the vase is important to you it might be the key to everything else."

"I don't know. When I saw it . . ." She frowned. "When I look at it I almost know. Then it's gone. But I know . . . I'm sure . . . I think it's mine. But I don't know."

Don't press.

"Well, we'll let it sit there. Maybe seeing it every day will push a button." I cracked two eggs into a bowl and added milk. "I made out a schedule for your pills. Can you handle it or do you want me to remind you?"

"Mmm?" she murmured, abstracted.

"The pills. Do you think you can remember to take them?"

She nodded, her gaze fixed on the vase, her lips pinched in concentration. Her mobile face reflected thoughts trudging laboriously behind her eyes.

She ate slowly, pausing once or twice, fork suspended halfway to her mouth. I drank my tea, waited for whatever would be forthcoming.

"Why did you bring me here?" she said suddenly, breaking the silence, startling me.

"Where else? I live here."

"I don't mean why here. I mean why anywhere? What made you . . . whatever . . . rescue? Why did you rescue me?"

"You and my daughter Laurie were friends. Best friends."

"Best friends?"

"Bosom buddies. All through high school. You spent more time at our place than you did at home."

She looked around the kitchen, frowning.

"Not here," I said. "We were in an apartment then. Downtown."

"I've never been here before?"

"No." I pushed away from the table. "I have to clean up the patio. Your cart is outside. Why don't you go through it, see if there's anything you want to keep."

"I'll get dressed." She hesitated. "Is it all right if I take a shower?"

"Of course, take a shower. You don't have to ask. Rub the salve onto your sores after you're finished, okay?"

She came out to the patio dressed in jeans and T-shirt, damp hair tied back with white string, eyes narrowed in her near-sighted attempt to see clearly.

"Your cart's over there." I pointed. "Garbage bags over here if you need them."

I turned back to my own mess. Stripping furniture is like baking: Two-thirds of your time is spent cleaning up after yourself. I tied a knot in a final garbage bag and looked up to see how Jenny was doing. She stood beside her cart, a dazed expression on her face, the ratty sweater she had worn dangling from one hand, the jeans from the other.

"Need help?" I asked.

"Help?" she echoed uncertainly. Her nose wrinkled. "This stuff stinks. Did I smell this bad?"

"Jenny, compared to the way you smelled that stuff is a romp through a rose garden."

"Oh," she said in a small voice.

"Come on." I reached for a fresh garbage bag. "We'll do it together."

With some reluctance she dropped the sweater into the bag, hesitated over the jeans, frowning, then reached into the rear pocket and withdrew a key. She held it in the palm of her hand, the frown deepening.

"Do you know what it's for?" I asked. "Or what it's to?"

She shook her head. "I've had it since . . . I've had it all the time. I don't know . . ."

"It'll come to you. Put it in your pocket and let's get on with this."

The first limp plastic bag from the cart contained a thin cotton towel in faded stripes of brown and green and yellow, wrapped around a worn nylon hairbrush with no handle, a toothbrush with splayed bristles, four plastic packets of various shampoo samples, a wad of paper napkins from a lunch counter dispenser, and a pitted-steel nail clipper.

I looked at Jenny. She shrugged uncertainly. I dropped it all into the garbage bag.

A flurry of fruit flies escaped when I loosened the top of the second bag. I caught a glimpse of green mold and the stench of rot and hastily retied the plastic handles.

The third bag was clothing, tightly packed. A pair of gray corduroy pants, frayed at the cuffs, napless at knees and seat. Two shabby sweaters, both garage sale rejects, one still with a spattering of beads and tarnished sequins, the other a coarse cableknit in an unpleasant shade of mustard. A faded navy duffle coat with a broken zipper and threadbare seams. Eleven unmatched socks. Two scarves, one at least six feet long, the other a square of shrunken wool. Brown knit mitts, raveled at the thumbs, and a pair of pile-lined black boots with run-down heels and pointed toes.

"You're not going to need any of this." I stuffed the boots back in the bag, dropped it in the cart, and piled the clothing on top. "Tomorrow's garbage day. Let's wheel the whole lot down to the street and let them haul it away, cart and all. Okay with you?"

Fright flashed momentarily in her eyes. Her fingers, reaching for the familiar, curled around the cart handle. She looked at me, blinking. Then she nodded. "Okay," she said.

I picked up my two garbage bags and took the paved walk circling the house. Jenny followed, dragging the cart behind her. We were placing them at the foot of the driveway when Larry arrived.

He tooted as he passed us by—*beep-de-beep-beep*—drove up to the house and parked, stepped from the car, and waited, a large brown paper bag cradled in his arms, a beatific smile on his face.

"*Bonjour, buenos días, guten tag,* hello. Also *shalom.*" He grinned at Jenny, fell into step behind her, and followed us into the house to the kitchen. "Have I got goodies for y'all or have I got goodies for y'all? Ask me."

He placed the paper bag on the kitchen table, reached in, and whipped out a bulky white deli bag.

"Smoked meat *sammidgis.* Dill pickles *mit* garlic. *Kebbitch* slaw. And strawberry cheesecake to die for."

He plunged his arm back into the brown bag. "And!" He glowed at Jenny, withdrew a clear plastic bag filled with video cassettes. "The glorious career of Jennifer Steele."

He dipped into the bag again and lifted out a shimmery black bag with gold rope for handles and a printed golden dragon rampant. "For you," he said. "I think . . ." His grin turned shy. "Anyway, I thought you needed something pretty."

Pretty wasn't the word for the kimono that emerged from the layers of black and gold tissue paper. Heavy silk in the deep vibrant blue of larkspur lavishly embroidered with ivory chrysanthemums, it was exquisite. And expensive.

"Put it on," Larry urged. "Cat? Would it be okay if I set up the VCR and we have lunch in the living room?"

I had forgotten how good Jenny was. Had been?

There were some thirty-odd commercials on the cassette, taped, Larry said, in chronological order, from the first for

Cranberry Crush in which a young, fresh Jenny walked barefoot on the sands of a misty sea, her splendid hair flowing in the wind, to one I had never seen, a perfume commercial featuring a sultry, languid Jenny with only two words scripted for that lush, husky voice. *Hi, babe.*

"Did you hear that?" Larry punched the mute button, then the reverse. "Hi, babe. Did you hear that? Two words and they get you right here." He stabbed a thumb in his abdomen. "That was the last one. You were doing *Halls* then. You were Amanda. Very sexy. You'd never done sexy before."

I glanced at Jenny. She was leaning forward, squinting at the speeded-up reverse action. Glasses. Tomorrow, glasses. Her eyelid was healing nicely.

"So, Jenny, what do you think?" Larry asked eagerly.

Jenny looked at him, frowning, her hand idly stroking the lustrous silk of the kimono sleeve. "Amanda?" she said, "who is Amanda?"

"You are. *Halls of Justice?* It's a soap opera. It's the last thing you did. You were Amanda Prentiss. They killed you off. Wrote you out. Whatever. You disappeared."

"When?"

"When? When were you Amanda? Or when did you disappear?"

"How long have I . . . when did I . . . get lost?"

"Almost a year. Your last *Halls* was November third. They killed you two weeks later. Last fall. November."

Jenny's frown deepened. She clasped her hands together, her fingers working. "That long," she muttered. "That long."

She looked up at me with bleak eyes. "Wasn't anybody looking for me?" she asked. "Don't I have a mother? A father? Brothers? Sisters? Any of those things?"

I hesitated. *Answer just the question.* Okay, Dan.

"You have a father. You have a stepmother. And you have two half brothers. Twins."

Her fingers stilled. "Why didn't . . ." she began, then, in a firmer voice demanded, "Where are they?"

"I don't know." I rose to my feet. "Look, why don't we

have the cheesecake in the kitchen? I'll make tea. And I'll tell you whatever I know for sure, okay?"

"Your mother died when you were nine. Cancer. I never knew her. When you and Laurie met you were a key kid. So was Laurie and you began coming home with Laurie after school. You were both twelve years old, your first year in junior high school."

I poured tea into three cups and handed one to Jenny. "With me so far?"

Jenny nodded.

"Your father remarried in spring, just before your thirteenth birthday. He married his secretary. She was six months pregnant when they were married. The twins were born in July. You stayed with us that summer."

"I did? Why?"

"Why?" I was taken aback by the question. "Well . . . it was . . . it seemed . . . I guess because . . ."

The hell with it, Dan. Sorry. I'll tell it the way it was, the way I saw it. She'll absorb what she can understand. That's what you told me about Laurie and sex, wasn't it?

"Your father was . . . is still, I suppose . . . a chemical engineer, Jenny. A . . . remote . . . man. Very rigid."

And one of the coldest human beings I've ever met. I'd come in contact with Oliver Steele on no more than four or five occasions and had never seen him smile. My most graphic memory of him is the odd way he stood, his glossy black shoes planted exactly parallel, a precise five inches apart. It's funny. I remember the feet. I can't recall the face.

"Your stepmother was a . . ." I veered away from the word. "Your stepmother wasn't what I'd call an empathetic character either. When her babies were born you became—sorry, Jen—you became excess baggage."

Jenny's shoulders hunched and I hastened to add, "Don't misunderstand me. There was no question of abuse. They seemed simply to ignore the fact of your existence. They never came to school plays, not even when you were the star.

They took the twins to Florida to visit her parents for Christmas the year you were fourteen. I have no idea what reason they gave you for leaving you behind. Anyway, that winter you stayed with us for the holidays."

The year you and Laurie discovered champagne.

"Shortly after you graduated—and they didn't show up then either—your father was transferred to the West Coast. I've forgotten where. If I ever knew. By then you had done a couple of commercials and you moved into an apartment with another actr—. . ."

It hit me like a bolt from the blue. I leapt from my chair, ran into the living room, and found my old and battered address book in the bottom drawer of my desk.

"What, Cat?" Larry was on his feet, Jenny wide-eyed, when I hurried back to the kitchen, leafing through the yellowed pages.

"Your agent! Hannah Peel! She should know . . ."

I found the number, dialed. "Why didn't I think of her before? She should be able to tell us something."

A honeyed voice answered on the third ring. "Silverhill Associates. Good afternoon. May I help you?"

"Yes. I'd like to speak to Hannah Peel, please."

There was a one-beat pause before the voice announced smoothly, "Ms. Peel is no longer with us. May I connect you with someone else?"

"Thank you, no. Could you tell me where Ms. Peel went? Where she is now?"

This time the pause extended to four beats. And this time the voice was human.

"Look. I'm sorry. I guess you didn't know. Ms. Peel is dead. I mean passed away. I'm sorry."

"When?"

"Last fall. November."

6

That's spooky," Larry said. "Hannah Peel died in November. Jennifer Steele disappeared in November. It's kind of spooky, isn't it?"

"It's probably sheer coincidence." I picked up my cup and carried it to the sink. I'd lost a good part of the day and Rafe's pieces were waiting to be varnished.

"I have to get back to work," I said. "Jenny? Maybe you should lie down for a while."

"I'm not really tired." Jenny was almost apologetic.

Larry brightened. "How about watching the unforgettable *Kiddy Korner* extravaganzas?" he asked. "Your insightful interpretation of that timeless icon, Miss Tidddleywinks? Or would you rather witness the breathtaking suspense of your great and glorious weather forecast period?"

"I don't know. Maybe . . ." Jenny faltered. "I can't . . ."

"Larry," I interrupted. "Jenny's nearsighted. We're going for glasses tomorrow. Why don't you wait until she can actually see all these wonders?"

"No problem." Larry brought his cup to the sink, rinsed it, and set it beside mine. "So. Maybe we can help you."

"Help me?"

"Varnishing. You do one piece. We do the other."

"Thanks, but no thanks." I smiled at him. A wide and innocent smile. "You really want to help?"

"I live to help. What do you want us to do?"

"Okay. For starters, clean up the lunch mess. Then empty the dishwasher and load in the dirty dishes. Strip Jenny's bed and put on clean sheets. Do the laundry. We're running out of sheets and towels. Still want to help?"

Larry grimaced at Jenny. "Make a note, Jen. Rule number one. Never volunteer."

I thought about Larry Mendelsohn as I applied the paste varnish and began the monotonous buffing required to restore a fine patina to the two antique pieces.

The night I met him, a little over a year ago, he had been savagely beaten by his lover, Luigi Caruso, a brutal man who died as violently as he had lived in a car bombing aimed at his organized crime boss.

Larry had been, among other things, a sometime picker for Charlie and Rafe, running to auctions, estate and garage sales, buying for Canterbury House Antiques.

"He has the eye," Rafe had said. "The innate taste. The lucky little bastard was born with an instinct the rest of us acquire only after we've put in years of trial and error. What he doesn't have is the knowledge antique dealers work bloody hard for. If Larry stopped flitting and combined the instinct with a solid base of knowledge he'd eventually make the rest of us look like rank amateurs."

A year ago, when Caruso died, Charlie had stepped in and, characteristically, had taken over.

"Just because you're gay, doesn't mean you have to be stupid," he had growled at Larry. "It's time you started using your brains instead of your butt. How many times have you been beaten up by those pricks you've been involved with? Twice? Three times? You know what your future looks like? AIDS or a wheelchair."

Charlie had patted Larry's swollen cheek.

"So, boychik. Here's what you do. You come into the shop a couple of hours every day. We'll teach you the trade. And, what the hell, even if you don't learn anything, you'll at least meet a better class of queers."

A sound from inside the house stilled my hand. I raised my head to listen.

Laughter. Joyful, bouncing laughter. And not just Larry. Jenny, too. Jenny was laughing.

I hadn't seen her even smile.

7

The next day, Friday, Charlie and Rafe were late. It was almost two when they arrived.

"Sorry, Cat," Rafe apologized, following Charlie into the kitchen. "Everything always takes longer than you expect. Axiom one."

"I know it well. Also axiom two: Nothing is ever as easy as you think it's going to be. No problem, Rafe. I hope you don't mind having leftover borscht for lunch?"

"Sour cream?" Charlie demanded.

"Of course. You want it hot or you want it cold?"

"Hot. Got anything for a salad?"

"If it's green I've got it. In the fridge. The Gallé and the Majorelle are on the patio. Don't you want to see them?"

"First things first. I'm starving." Charlie swung the fridge door wide. "Rafe, go look."

I turned the heat on under the borscht and got out of Charlie's way. My kitchen shrinks when he's in it and it's not because he's over six feet with a body like an aging Arnold Whatsisname. Charlie's ebullience displaces a lot of air. He fills a room.

"The estate appraisal?" I asked. "Anything worthwhile?"

Charlie shrugged. "Some decent Gouda, several paintings of the cows-in-the-field school, and a shitload of furniture. Rafe traded our appraisal fee for a cabinet-on-stand he wants to talk to you about."

Rafe, coming in from the patio, heard. "It's Flemish," he said. "Mahogany, beautiful carving. The varnish has crazed and gone milky and one of the drawer pulls is missing. Want to take it on? We'd like it for a show we're doing at the beginning of October."

"How big is it? If the weather changes I'll have to move to the basement and big stuff won't go down the stairs."

"The cabinet can be separated from the stand. Shouldn't be a problem. We pick it up Monday. We'll drop it off here if you can take it on."

"Sure. That'll be fine."

Rafe nodded, smiled his one-sided smile. "You do good work, Cat. The Gallé is superb."

Charlie, tearing spinach for the salad, snorted. "Twit. Her price just went up." He winked at me with his one golden eye. "So where's Orphan Annie?"

"Off to lunch with Larry. They should be back soon. And her name is Jenny. Jennifer Steele."

"Steele? Jennifer Steele? Isn't there an actress by that name?" He frowned at Rafe. "That girl we thought was so good, the townie who was gang-raped in that PBS movie? Wasn't her name Jennifer Steele?"

Rafe nodded. "And if our bag lady is really Jennifer Steele it explains Larry. He's twittering around with a silly grin on his face. Hasn't heard word one. We just assumed he'd fallen in love again."

"He's been coming here," I said. "And speaking of Larry, he bought Jenny an expensive robe. Much too expensive. You can't be paying him enough for him to afford things from The Golden Dragon."

"Pay Larry?" Charlie grinned at me. "Hell, Cat. We don't pay Larry. We educate him."

"You don't pay him?" I said blankly. "So where does he get the money to buy pure silk, hand-embroidered, five-hundred-dollar kimonos? He dresses out of the Salvation Army. He drives that funny little car. What's he using for money?"

Charlie's grin expanded. "Funny little car? Cat, Larry probably paid more for that funny little car than you did for this rinky-dink house of yours."

"Rinky-dink!"

"Hey," Charlie growled. "I was being kind. You've got stone, you've got a tacked-on stucco kitchen, you've got sideboard and brick additions, you've got windows at every level and no two the same. This house is an abortion perpetrated by three generations of blind architects. The only saving grace is the cedar hedge; at least your neighbors don't have their tender sensibilities offended."

"Too damn bad about their sensibilities. *Rinky-dink!*" I snorted. "This house has character. It's mine and I love it just the way it is, warts and all."

"So do I." Charlie chortled at getting my goat. "Anytime you want to sell I'll give you double whatever you paid."

"Forget it, Chuck." He hates being called Chuck. "So how does he do it? Larry? Is he printing his own money?"

Charlie gave the salad a final toss and carried the bowl to the table.

"Lay on the borscht, Cat. We'll tell you the tale of Larry Mendelsohn while we eat."

"Larry's paternal grandparents," Charlie began, then stabbed at a chunk of green pepper in his salad, "the Mendelsohns, were graduates of the Warsaw ghetto and Auschwitz. Eventually they wound up here, made a life, had a child. A son. They named him Markus, after a brother who didn't survive the Warsaw ghetto uprising."

Charlie chewed on the green pepper, laid down his fork, picked up his spoon, and stirred his borscht.

"Now, the Mendelsohns worked very, very hard." Charlie adopted the inflections of the storyteller. "And Markus, who was not only very bright but also very beautiful, grew up and went to law school where he met his future wife who was also very bright and very beautiful." The teller-of-tales cadence ended and Charlie added wryly, "Also very Gentile. Also very rich. Her name was Nora Woodward."

"Woodward? Distilleries? *Those* Woodwards?"

"The same." Charlie spooned soup into his mouth.

"Where did you hear all this?"

Rafe answered. "From Larry, where else? He stayed with us for a couple of weeks last year. After the Caruso thing. He wasn't in great shape, if you remember."

I nodded. "Go on. Markus married Nora."

"I imagine the Mendelsohns weren't initially ecstatic over a *shiksa* daughter-in-law. Given their history. But they liked Nora and they loved their son. They took her to their bosom. Bosoms, plural? Whatever. The Woodwards. The Woodwards were something else again."

He stopped. "My soup's getting cold. Rafe, you tell Cat about the Woodwards. I can't talk and eat."

Rafe pushed his empty plate aside and rested his elbows on the table.

"The Woodwards have been customers of ours for years," he said. "They collect Victorian brilliant-cut glass."

He frowned. "Never thought of it before. What else would they collect? They're brilliant-cut people. Handsome, and I mean both of them. Silver foxes. Tall and rich and thin. Old money. Old family. Old school."

"Quintessential WASPs, he means," Charlie mumbled over a mouthful of salad.

"Bone-marrow bigots is what I mean," Rafe said bluntly. "You know the type, Cat. The eyes glaze over. The well-bred manners are suddenly exquisitely well-bred. Blew our minds when Larry told us they were his grandparents."

"So I assume the Woodwards didn't take somebody with a name like Markus Mendelsohn to their plural bosoms?"

"Bosoms?" Charlie snorted. "Any ten-year-old boy has bigger boobs than Grace Woodward. What bosoms?"

"Nora was their only offspring." Rafe ignored Charlie. "I imagine they gritted their teeth and endured. Larry was four when it happened. He only knows whatever his old nanny told him about what it was like before."

"What happened?"

"Evidently old man Mendelsohn had a sister, also a camp survivor, living in Israel. It seems she didn't have long to go and the Mendelsohns wanted to spend what was possibly her last Yom Kippur with her. Markus and Nora went along. They were only to be gone a week and they left Larry with the housekeeper and Mume Sarah. Mume Sarah was his nanny."

"She wasn't his aunt," Charlie interjected. When I frowned at him, confused, he added, "*Mume* is Hebrew for aunt. She wasn't his aunt. She wasn't anybody's aunt. They just called her Mume Sarah."

"Oh. Okay. So what happened?"

"This was all in October 1973," Rafe said. He looked at me expectantly. The date meant nothing to me.

"The Yom Kippur War, Cat. They were in a kibbutz near Golan Heights when the war started. All four died when a direct hit destroyed the bus they were in."

The words had dropped like stones. We sat in an echoing silence. Then Charlie, busily gathering our empty plates, continued.

"The Woodwards took Larry." He carried the dishes to the sink. "The first thing they did was get rid of Mume Sarah. I guess two Jews under their roof was one Jew too many."

"Two too many." There was contempt in Rafe's voice.

"Yeah. Right." Charlie plugged in the kettle and reached into the cupboard for tea bags. "So Larry grew up in boarding schools and summer camps. On the rare occasions he was home the servants took over. He barely knew his grandparents. He knew next to nothing about his parents. There were pictures of his mother around the house. None of his father."

Charlie slammed cups down on the table.

"Those frigid fuckers," he said angrily. "What did they expect? What the hell did they expect?"

I looked at Rafe. He shrugged.

"Larry was caught bare-assed with another boy. He was fifteen. The other kid was seventeen. They were expelled, both of them."

"Woodward went to the school and got Larry." Charlie had cooled off. "And this is the part you're not going to believe, Cat. He didn't speak to the kid. Not one word in a two-hour drive. He took him straight to a building in town. Up the elevator. Into a lawyer's office. He said, and these are his exact words, according to Larry, 'This is Larry. I want the little Jew fag out of my house. Now. Arrange it.' And he walked out."

"You're right, Charlie," I said, stunned. "I don't believe it."

Charlie nodded. "I know. Anyway, it seems this lawyer is the executor or the trustee or whatever they're called, of the

Mendelsohn estate. So, he rents an apartment. He hires Mume Sarah back as a housekeeper. He gets Larry enrolled in a local high school. And this is when Larry finds out he's got money coming out the old wazoo. Money from the Mendelsohns. Money from his father. Money from his mother. Lots and lots of money from his mother." Charlie tilted his head at Rafe. "How much do you think Larry has? One million? Two million?"

Rafe shrugged. "Three million? Four?" He glanced at his watch. "We better get on our horses, Charlie. Gordon has an appointment at four. He'll close the shop if we're not back."

I followed them to the van, Charlie carrying the Gallé, Rafe the Majorelle.

"What do you want me to do with the candle stand?"

"Keep it? Throw it away? Burn it?" Rafe lovingly wrapped the Majorelle in a quilted blanket and placed it in the van. "It's garbage."

He was sliding the van door closed when Larry's silver car turned in from the street, skimmed up the driveway, and came to rest beside my wagon. Larry and Jenny stepped out.

"Well, good golly Miss Molly," Charlie murmured. "It's the Bobbsey Twins."

From their new, identically sculpted haircuts to gray snakeskin boots, they were dressed alike. Aviator glasses with silvery rims. Gray leather jackets, black turtlenecks, black jeans tucked into the expensive boots. In the unisex clothing they were clones, their resemblance striking. We stared, Charlie, Rafe, and I.

The uncertain expression on Jenny's face as they neared made me see us through her eyes.

Charlie, pushing sixty, in his black Edwardian jacket with a rosebud in the lapel, a black patch on one eye, the other a wicked golden hazel. The salt-and-pepper mane of hair. The black Vandyke beard hiding his once-shattered jaw.

Rafe, twenty years younger, with his ruined face, one side pitted and scarred, the other a Michelangelo portrait. The drooping eyelid on the frozen side of his face gives him a faintly sinister air, his half-smile seems sardonic.

I'm no prize either. The oversize shirts I wear are usually paint- and stripper-stained, my jeans rump-sprung. I'm sixty-two and it's beginning to show. Major wrinkling has been mercifully delayed but the chin is sagging. Most days I forget to put on makeup. Most days I pull my hair back with a rubber band and forget it.

"Just arriving or just leaving?" Larry asked sunnily.

"Leaving. And we're late." Rafe nodded at Jenny, thanked me for lunch, circled the van, and climbed into the driver's seat. "Let's go, Charlie."

"Yassa, massa." Charlie smiled at Jenny. "Looking good there, Annie."

We watched the van back down the driveway.

"Who are they?" Jenny said as it turned into the street, Charlie's arm flapping good-bye from the window.

I looked at her, startled. "They own the antique shop where you found the vase. You don't remember them?"

"I vaguely remember . . . I guess I didn't see . . ." She touched her cheek. "What happened to him?"

"Rafe? His name's Rafael Verdoni, by the way. Gay bashers is what happened to him. They were climbing all over Rafe. Charlie tried to help. That's how and when they met. Rafe was dragged facedown across a cement parking lot. Charlie got himself a few broken ribs and his jaw smashed. And he lost an eye. That eye patch isn't just window dressing."

Somewhat subdued, Jenny and Larry followed me into the house, into the kitchen.

"I thought you were only going for an eye test, to get a prescription for glasses," I said.

Larry answered. "We went to the Whatsitsname, you know, where they do it all in an hour? What do you think of them, the glasses?"

"Very nice. They suit you, Jen. Tell me what you paid, Larry. I'll write you a check. For the clothes, too."

"Not necessary, Cat. We worked it all out," Larry said. "See, the way we figure, Jennifer Steele must have a bank account somewhere. When Jen remembers where, she can pay me back. Doesn't that make sense to you?"

I looked at Jenny. "Make sense to you?"

She shrugged. "I guess. But I don't know where he gets all this 'we' stuff. I say no. He says yes. I say no. So he says . . ." She looked at Larry with smiling eyes. "He says if I say no again, he'll strip and streak the mall."

Larry grinned back at her. "Whatever it takes," he said. "Cat? Is it okay if we watch *Kiddy Korner?*"

"Of course it's okay. From now on. Don't even ask. *Mi casa es su casa.* Okay?"

"Right on. Thanks, Cat."

I watched the first half hour with them—Jenny, Miss Tiddleywinks, in a pink smock, ponytail, and bangs, fresh face bare of makeup, the girl next door, the baby-sitter every young mother dreams of finding—then went out to the patio to dismantle Irving's game table in preparation for stripping.

Two hours later it was Jenny the weather forecaster, crisp and professional in a blue blazer, her hair falling sleekly from a center part to just below her earlobes, face skillfully made-up to emphasize her expressive eyes and bearing little resemblance to sweet Miss Tiddleywinks. Only the magical voice was the same.

I asked Larry if he had a copy of the TV movie Charlie had mentioned.

"The PBS one? Sure. Got it right here."

"Why don't you stay for dinner? I'll call out for pizza. Throw together a Caesar salad. We can set up in the living room and watch while we eat. You're not too tired, Jen?"

"No. I'm fine."

The movie started euphorically. Blue skies, red and gold autumn trees, ivied college walls, rolling campus. The love story of a football jock and a cheerleader, both beautiful. When Jenny appeared I didn't recognize her.

"There she is." Larry pointed. "There you are, Jen."

She's a waitress in the local hangout bar and grill. She peers at the world from under an untamed mane of kinky red hair. She's stoop-shouldered and graceless, a lusterless creature shlepping beer and Cokes and coffee to the rowdy football behemoths and their

Barbie Doll pom-pom girls. Her name is Shelley. Born Shirley.

I glanced at Jenny. "Ring any bells?" I asked.

She shook her head. "No bells. Larry keeps saying 'There you are, that's you,' but I'm looking at strangers."

On screen the plot thickens. The home team wins, yay. The heroes descend on the bar and grill, drunk as lords. To the victors go the spoils. Rape the peasants.

Jenny's talent is impressive as the slow-witted Shelley begins to realize there is nothing good-natured about the butt-and-bosom grabbing she is being subjected to. Pressed against the bar by a grunting, groping bully, she fights, bites deeply into his arm. He punches her and she falls, cracking her head on the brass footrail.

Squealing and screaming from the pom-pom girls, some of whom depart. Including the cheerleader who tries, in vain, to convince the football hero to leave with her.

Gang bang. Closeup on Jenny's—Shelley's—bloodied face, her screams and pleading drowned in a thundering sound track. On and on.

It's all over the campus, groups of students whispering, dissolving, regrouping. Confrontation between the Cheerleader and the Hero. Did he or didn't he? He denies. Can she believe him? How can she know for sure? The theme music swells.

Angst. Lots of angst.

They're going to buy Shelley off, those monied morons. Ten thousand dollars. No charges laid.

Silence. The music track is stilled. Shelley sits on a hospital bed, her bandaged head bowed. As the camera dollies in she raises her head. Her cheek is bruised, her eye swollen shut. There are stitches . . .

Jenny leapt to her feet, her TV tray flying. "That's me," she cried. She was trembling. "That's me."

8

I was in a hospital bed," Jenny said. "That's the first thing I remember."

We sat, the three of us, at the kitchen table. Jenny's hands were clasped around her coffee mug but she was calm.

"They told me I was brought in the night before. I'd been hit by a car. A hit-and-run. I had a head concussion and a sprained wrist. My shoulder had been dislocated. A lot of bruises. They said I looked worse than I actually was. They asked me what my name was."

She looked at me, at Larry. "It's a weird sensation. Drawing a complete blank like that. One of the nurses gave me a mirror. I saw that girl in the movie, Shelley. The head bandage. Black eye. The bruises. But the face in that mirror didn't mean a thing to me."

She raised her mug, hesitated. She frowned, collecting her memory into sequence.

"Then the police came. They asked my name, where did I live, where had I been, where had I been going, had I seen the car that hit me, why didn't I have any identification, had I had a purse with me? All I could say was I don't know, I don't know. Then the hospital people told me I was in the emergency ward. I couldn't stay. I'd have to leave."

"Leave?" Larry's face was incredulous. "They were just going to throw you out in the street?"

Jenny shook her head. "Apparently the police had made arrangements with a social worker to pick me up and take me to a women's shelter. The nurse who'd given me the mirror brought my clothes and helped me put them on. She took me down to the lobby. 'Sit here.' She parked me in one of the chairs beside the front desk cubicle. 'Shouldn't be long.' "

Jenny snorted. "Ever sit on one of those molded plastic chairs for any length of time? With a sore butt? I sat. I stood. I hobbled around that damn lobby, my knee was killing me. I checked out my pockets. Nothing in the jacket, a down-filled parka sort of thing. I found the key." Jenny gestured toward the dishwasher where the key lay beside the black vase, "and a folded twenty-dollar bill in the pocket of my jeans. That was it, that was all."

"No watch? No jewelry?" Larry frowned. "What about your glasses?"

"No glasses. No nothing." Jenny shrugged. "So I waited. I don't know how long. But I watched it get dark outside. The streetlights, the car lights. It was night out there. Then that nurse came by. 'You still here?' she said. 'You should have been gone hours ago!'

"She went into the cubicle where the reception desk was. I could see the receptionist shake her head. The nurse made a phone call and came back to me.

" 'Car trouble,' she said. 'The woman who was supposed to pick you up had car trouble. They want you to come there. It isn't far, two or three blocks. Go down the steps, turn left. When you get to Powell Street, turn right. It's the second house from the corner. Number three-nine-zero-six. Remember that because it's just an ordinary house, no sign. Three-nine-zero-six. They're waiting for you.'

"I hope they're not still waiting." Jenny's voice was weary. "Because I never found the house. I never even found Powell Street. I asked a couple of people and got sent off in six directions. I couldn't find the street. I couldn't even find the hospital again. I couldn't keep walking. I was cold and hungry and I hurt like hell. I found a greasy spoon and ate the world's worst hamburger."

Jenny rested her chin in her hands, her elbows braced on the table. She was obviously tiring.

"I must have fallen asleep," she continued. "The next thing I knew, somebody rapped me on the sore shoulder. I woke up, like fast. And there's this grungy old guy in a dirty apron. He's got sour, tired eyes and a toothpick stuck in the corner of his mouth. 'You can't sleep here, lady,' he says, so I ask for another cup of coffee. He looks me over with those dead eyes. 'You don't want no more coffee,' he says after a long stare. 'Listen, kid. Go to the corner booth. Lie down on the bench. Nobody's gonna see you there.' He jerks his thumb to the rear of the place. 'But you gotta be outta here before the boss gets here in the morning.' "

Jenny removed her glasses and rubbed her eyes with the heels of her palms. "Damn," she said. "I'm fading."

I stood up. "Save the rest for tomorrow. Want help?"

She shook her head, pushed herself up from her chair. "I can make it." She smiled wanly. "G'night, kids," she said and tottered off down the hall to bed.

Larry, half risen from his chair, sat down and watched her go, his face anxious.

"Is she all right?" he asked.

"She will be. In the morning."

"Cat? Uh . . ." He ducked his head. "Could I . . . do you suppose I could stay over? If you'd rather I didn't that's okay, too," he added.

"If you don't mind the living room couch."

Unfamiliar sounds dragged me up from the depths of heavy sleep. Mewling? Stirring? A cry? Before I could sort them out I fell back into a nightmare of Laurie, pursued by amorphous, faceless monsters.

I awoke fully this time, heart pounding.

Pale light glowed on the ceiling, reflecting from the hall. I glanced at the radio alarm, three-ten, and forced myself out of my snug eiderdown cocoon.

The light, softly luminous, came from Jenny's room, from a peach-glow fairy lamp on the bureau near the open door.

In a rocking chair beside the bed was Larry, his arm outstretched, holding Jenny's hand. Both slept.

I brought a blanket from the hall closet, covered him, and went back to bed.

9

Okay, now, here we go." Larry pushed his plate aside, his omelet half eaten. *"Life on the Street* starring Jennifer Steele. Tell us what it was like, Jen."

We were out on the patio, eating the brunch Larry had prepared. I had already put in three hours on Irving's game table before Jenny and Larry wakened to the perfect Indian summer day.

The air was unseasonably mellow, fragrant with the winey scents of autumn. Above us, the cloudless sky was a milky blue, the sun golden through the bronzing foliage of the oak tree. Once in a while a fat bumble bee rumbled by on its route to a bed of asters, blooming pink and mauve beside the house. A crow called raucously. A yellowing leaf spiralled lazily, then swooped to a perfect landing on Jenny's plate.

She picked it up and stroked it with a gentle finger. "There isn't much to tell," she said.

Larry's disappointment was obvious.

"No, really." She shook her head. "There isn't. Life narrows down to finding somewhere to sleep, something to eat, and a toilet."

Larry's grin was startled. "A toilet?"

"John. Can. Potty," Jenny said drily. "Pooping in a windy alley in the dead of winter is a shitty way to go, believe me. If I hadn't met Doris I'd have probably become a devout anal retentive."

Larry's smile broadened. "Who's Doris?" he asked.

Jenny dropped the leaf to the ground. She rested her elbows on the table, her chin supported on a closed fist.

"Doris. Doris is . . . was . . ." She interrupted herself. "I was standing on a street corner wondering which way to go. Major decision. I'm standing there and out of the blue this woman grabs me by the sleeve and starts screeching. She's got a voice like a banshee, she's got a fistful of my jacket, and she isn't letting go and I'm trying to shake her loose and I'm dragging her and she's dragging this dumb cart and I'm starting to panic."

"Man. Scarey." Larry urged her on.

"Scarey?" Jenny was surprised at the word. "I wasn't scared. You know what I was? I was *embarrassed*, for God's sake. Me? Who hadn't bathed or brushed my teeth or my hair for at least five days? My clothes looked as if I'd slept in them, which of course I had. I was dirty and I didn't have a dime. And I was embarrassed by this woman attached to me and giving me hell at the top of her lungs?"

"What was she giving you hell for?" I asked.

"Because I hadn't called her. Not on her birthday. Not at Christmas. Not at Easter. Not even on Mother's Day."

I was intrigued. "Who did she think you were?"

"That day? I was her daughter that day. Later I got to be all of them. Daughter Patty. Sister Lizzie. Bonnie, her daughter-in-law. Even Debbie, her baby-sitter."

"How old was she? Doris?"

Jenny frowned. "It's hard to say. Fifty-something? Her hair was white. One of her eyes had gone milky. Her evil eye, she said. If she turned on the power she could paralyze me just by looking at me."

"Crazy," Larry said.

"Crazy as a bedbug. But she knew where the soup kitchens were. She knew which bakery handed out stale bread and which restaurant let you pick over plates of leftovers before they scraped them into the garbage. And she had a place."

"What's a place?" Larry looked at me questioningly. I shrugged.

"A place is a place. Somewhere to sleep," Jenny explained. "She had a room at the Jesus Saves Hotel."

"The what?"

Jenny grinned. "It's a boarded-up old dump. Evidently it had been a Pentecostal church at some time in its history and the Jesus Saves sign survived. So that's what the squatters called it, what else? The place was always full of drifters, coming and going. Doris had been there a couple of years. She had a room in the basement. She kept it locked with a padlock that must've come off the ark.''

I glanced at the dishwasher. "Maybe that's what that key is for? The padlock?"

Jenny shook her head. "She never trusted me with a key. That key has to be for some other lock."

"What was it like? Her room?" Larry asked.

"Four old mattresses, stacks of newspapers, piles of old clothes, and a rusty barbecue she'd liberated from a garbage dump somewhere."

"What'd she want a barbecue for?"

"Burning newspapers. Or any wood we could find. There was no heat. The building had been abandoned and condemned. No heat. No electricity. No water. It was just a place."

"Would Doris still be there? Now?" Larry asked.

Jenny shook her head. "They're both gone. Doris and the Jesus Saves Hotel."

"What do you mean, *gone*? Gone where? When?"

"The Jesus Saves . . . I don't know . . . March? April? You never know what day it is, never mind which month. I know it was in spring, the weather was getting warmer. The police raided the place. It seems someone was running a crackhouse on the top floor."

"Really?" Larry was fascinated. "Did you know about it?"

Jenny shrugged. "I never thought about it."

"But didn't you see them coming and going?"

Jenny studied him, her expression remote. "They're all coming and going," she said finally. "Crackheads and winos and schizos and runaways. You don't see because you don't look. Something to eat and somewhere to sleep. That's all there is."

Larry nodded, subdued. "So what happened to Doris?"

"After the Jesus Saves was bulldozed we hauled our carts around, slept where we could. Parks, alleys, wherever. Panhandling. We pooled whatever we got until Doris began accusing me of holding out on her."

Jenny shrugged. "I can't really blame her. I wasn't tracking too well by then. I'd forget what I was supposed to be doing. I'd sit down for a rest somewhere and fall asleep."

"The anemia," I said.

"I guess. Anyway, that's when I got to be Bonnie. The daughter-in-law? She told me she'd never liked me. Said I'd turned her son against her, made her grandchildren hate her. She told me if I didn't stay clear of her she'd turn on the megapower of her evil eye and fry me dead."

"What happened to her? You said she was gone."

"I never saw her again. She just sort of disappeared."

Inside the house the phone rang. I pushed away from the table, touched Jenny's shoulder as I passed. "No more till I get back, okay?"

It was Mike Melnyk.

"So what did you think of Hawaii?" I asked.

"Hawaii!" He spat the word. I smiled to myself and sat back for what I knew was coming. "Paradise Lost. Disneyland on a raft. McDonalds-on-the-Pacific. Plastic grass skirts, for Christ's sake. We've desecrated Eden, Cat. The kindest thing we could do for Hawaii is cut it loose and let it float away."

"Uh-huh," I said, when he paused. "Sounds like you had a wonderful time. Would you like to come for dinner and tell me about it?"

"Not tonight. I just got in an hour ago and I'm pooped. I'm going to bed. Tomorrow?"

"Sure."

"Cat? Can we have meat loaf? I've eaten enough fruits and vegetables and fish and rice to last the rest of my life. My soul is crying out for meat loaf. Meat loaf and creamed corn and scalloped potatoes."

"Good, Lord, Mike. The calories. The cholesterol."

"The hell with cholesterol. I lost ten pounds out there and I want them back."

I said good-bye, replaced the phone in its cradle, and went back out to the patio.

"That was Mike Melnyk," I said to Larry. "Remember him?"

Larry smiled. "Oh, yes. I remember Mike."

Jenny's head swivelled from Larry to me. "Who is Mike Melnyk?" she asked.

"Mike? He's a good friend. He's an ex-newspaperman, a police reporter. He wrote a popular column at one time, too. I think you'll like him."

"You'll like him, Jen." Larry nodded. "He's a really sharp old guy."

Old guy? Mike is my age, sixty-two. I let it pass. I guess at twenty-nine, anyone past fifty is over the hill.

"He's coming for dinner tomorrow night." I frowned at Irving's game table. "Damn. I was hoping to get a first coat on that thing today."

"So what's the problem?" Larry asked.

"Mike wants meat loaf. I'll have to go get groceries."

Larry stood up. "No big deal," he said. "Make a list. I'll go shopping. You work on the table. Jen can have a nap. Then I'll take us to La Mer and we'll pig out on lobster."

10

Next morning I finished the game table to the sound of church bells from the nearby seminary. Somewhere, someone was burning leaves and the wistful autumn smell filled me with a gentle melancholy. I put the table into the station wagon and went into the house, grateful to have it to myself.

Larry had arrived early that morning, unexpected.

"I'm going picking for Charlie and Rafe," he explained. "The Beth Tikvah Bazaar and a Sunday flea market. I thought Jen might like to come along."

Jenny had liked. They'd whisked away in that expensive kiddy car of his. Any car that cost more than my house should seat more than two people.

I selected *Fiddler on the Roof*, the perfect music for my mood, slipped the CD into the player, and peeled potatoes and onions to the yearning lyrics of "Sunrise, Sunset."

Mike clomped into the kitchen at four-thirty, a package wedged under his arm.

"Smells good in here," he announced. He set the package on the counter, looked at me, and smiled that clown's grin of his. His month in Hawaii had provided a deep tan and the ten pounds he lost had come off the squirrel pouch he developed after he quit smoking.

"So," he said, "how's it been going?"

"Good. I gather you didn't enjoy your holiday."

He shrugged. "I'm like fine wine. I don't travel well."

"Fine wine made from sour grapes." I kissed his mahogany cheek. "But I missed you anyway. Welcome home."

"Thanks." He pushed the package to me. "Here. I brought you something."

"Aw, Mike. That was nice. Thank you."

I ripped away the paper and opened the box to reveal a printed cotton something that looked like an explosion in a paint factory. Red and green parrots. Yellow and brown pineapples. Huge pink and purple flowers. I blinked at it.

"It's a muumuu," Mike explained. "The clerk said everybody buys them to take back to the mainland. What's the matter? Don't you like it?"

The sound of the front door opening and closing saved me from answering. Jenny and Larry sauntered into the kitchen.

"Mike, you remember Larry. Larry Mendelsohn?" I said.

Mike nodded. "Hey, Larry. Good to see you," he said and frowned at Jenny. "I know you, don't I? Do I know you?"

"You've seen her on TV," Larry said, pleased.

"Yeah. That's right." Mike's face cleared. "You used to do the weather didn't you?"

Larry laughed. "Used to do the weather? Mike, this is Jennifer Steele."

"Never knew the name. Jennifer Steele?" Mike's brows drew together. "Wait a minute. Jennifer Steele? Wasn't there something . . . I read something. Last year sometime?" He rapped the table with his knuckles. "Damn, I never forget a name," he said irritably. "Jennifer Steele. Weren't you mixed up in some sort of killing or something? Maybe a year ago?"

We froze, the three of us. Jenny, Larry, and I.

"What?" Mike glared at me, at the others. "What?"

"Mike," I said. "Are you sure?"

"Sure of what? That I read something? Sure I'm sure. Sure of what it is I read? No. But I can track it down."

"How?"

"Newspaper files. You should know that, Cat." He glanced at Jenny. "Why? She won't tell you?"

We sat down to dinner and told Mike everything we knew about Jenny, everything she knew. Larry filled in the career details, I provided the rest. Mike ate hungrily, asked for a second helping. When he finished, he pushed his plate aside, leaned his elbows on the table, and eyed Jenny.

"I don't get what you were doing here," he said. "You lived in New York, worked in New York. You have no family here and, other than Cat, the way I see it, no friends here. What the hell were you doing here?"

"I don't know." Jenny looked at me helplessly. She was pale and beginning to tire. "I just don't know."

I put my hand over hers. "Don't let the way Mike talks intimidate you, Jen. He used to be a newspaperman. He can't do subtle." A thought occurred to me. "Maybe you were here because of Hannah?"

"Hannah?" Mike snapped. "Who's Hannah?"

"Hannah Peel. Jenny's agent. She died last November."

"Died?" Mike pounced on the word. "How did she die?"

"I didn't ask. I was so stunned when they told me she was dead I didn't think to ask. But I'll tell you one thing. For sure, Jenny had nothing to do with it. If that's what you're insinuating."

"I'm not insinuating anything," Mike said. "I asked a simple question: How did she die? That's insinuating?"

"Hey, don't bite my head off," I protested. "We don't know. That's the simple answer to your simple question. We don't know."

Mike nodded. "Okay," he said, satisfied. He nodded once more, decisively. "Okay. Tomorrow I'll go down to the *Gazette* and go through the microfiles. November narrows it down. We should get at least a couple of answers." He smiled at Jenny. "You okay, kid?" he asked gently.

She warmed to that clownish grin. I felt her hand relax under mine. "Bloody," she conceded. "But unbowed."

" 'Atta girl." Mike pushed away from the table. "Cat, I hate to eat and run but my body clock's still out of whack. If I don't get home to bed right now you're going to have to scrape me off the floor."

I walked him to his car.

"Seems like a nice kid," he commented. "You notice the resemblance between those two?"

"I noticed."

"Thanks for the dinner. It was great."

He turned the ignition key and the motor coughed to life. "Gotta get the damn thing tuned," he grunted. "G'night, Cat. I'll call you as soon as I have some answers."

11

I awoke, headachy and arthritic, to the steady drizzle of September rain. Damn. I'd have to work in the basement. I hooked my leg over the mattress edge, yanked myself out of bed, showered and dressed quietly, and went to the kitchen to prepare breakfast.

Coffee was perking cheerfully, sending out a life-giving aroma, when the doorbell emitted a single *bleep*. Feeling put upon and cranky, I went to see who was invading my territory at eight in the morning.

It was Larry. He stood hunched under the dripping eaves, smiling wetly, a paper bag in either hand.

"Oh, for Pete's sake," I said crossly. "Come on in. Are you on your way to work?"

"I'm not going in today." He followed me to the kitchen, set the damp brown bags on the counter. "I picked up fresh croissants and wild strawberry jam. The croissants should still be warm." He eyed me warily. "You mad at me?"

"Mad at you? No, I'm not mad at you. I'm mad at the whole damn dripping world. Take off your jacket. Hang it on the doorknob. And get yourself a towel out of the second drawer there. Your hair's sopping wet." I slammed two coffee mugs on the table. "So? Why aren't you going to work?"

"Jenny's contacts." He scrubbed his head with a towel. "We ordered contact lenses last week. They should be ready this morning." He dropped the towel around his neck. "I came early because I thought we could deliver the game table for you when we go to pick up the contacts."

Oh, hell. How can you be snarky with someone who insists on being nice? I thanked him, sent him to waken Jenny, and laid out breakfast for three.

They left, taking my car. I went down to the basement to tidy my workroom, untouched since spring. I listed supplies I would need and then returned upstairs to make a couple of phone calls, Dan Freedman first.

"He's in bed with the flu," Marcie answered. "Anything I can do?"

"Thanks, Marcie. It's not urgent. He told me to call him today. About Jenny. That's all."

"Right. Let's see here. She has medication for another eight days, so you're okay there. Dan'll be back before then. Just keep doing what you're doing. How is she?"

"Great. No more blackouts. Eating well, sleeping a lot."

"Good. She remember anything yet?"

"Just the last few months. Nothing before."

"It'll come. Gotta go now." She hung up.

I was dialing Rena, a friend from the flea market days, to inquire about antique drawer pulls when the doorbell rang, *beep-de-beep-beep*, Charlie and Rafe announcing their arrival. I hung up and met them maneuvering a tall cabinet-on-stand into the foyer. Rafe was snarling, "Gently, Charlie, goddammit. *Gently*. Cat? Where do you want it?"

"Put it in the living room for now. You're sure it comes apart?"

"It comes apart," Rafe gritted through his teeth. "All you need is a screwdriver. Right, Charlie? Just a simple old screwdriver."

"So I forgot the screwdriver. Sue me," Charlie snapped. "Cat? You got a screwdriver handy?"

"Forget the screwdriver," I protested. "Just get it into the living room. I'll take it apart myself."

"I'm not going to use it on the goddamn cabinet," Charlie snarled. "I'm gonna unscrew Rafe's belly button and let his goddamn arse fall off."

I snickered. Rafe's glare relented. He smiled crookedly.

"Aw, what the hell," he said. "Sorry, Cat. Those stupid bastards tried to renege on the cabinet deal. I think Max was out there and got to them. Plus it's Monday, it's raining, and we're running late. Okay, Charlie. I'll get off your back. So let's move the fucking cabinet, okay?"

They wrestled the cabinet into the living room.

"No time for coffee?" I asked when it was in place.

"Not today, thanks Cat," Rafe said, brushing his hands.

"I see Larry's car is here." Charlie thumbed toward the driveway outside. "When you take the cabinet apart and remove all the drawers it'll be easy to handle. Larry can help you carry it down to the basement."

Their gray van had barely vanished into the gray veil of misty rain when my car raced up the driveway and came to a screeching halt that sent my shoulders up to my ears. Larry leapt from the driver's seat and ran to the house, followed by Jenny, her face radiant with excitement.

"The key!" Larry burst into the foyer. "Jenny's key!"

"It's on the dishwasher." I stepped aside hastily. He rushed past me and I asked Jenny, "What's happening?"

"I remembered my address!" Her eyes were an incandescent blue. "Eleven-seventy Kensington. I *remembered!*"

"Cat?" Larry called from the kitchen. "Do you know where Kensington is?"

"Hold on a sec." I went to the living room and dug out the city street guide from my desk drawer.

"We were picking up the lenses." Larry was at my elbow. "They were filling out the insurance forms and they asked Jenny for her address. She said eleven-seventy Kensington. Just like that she said eleven-seventy Kensington."

"It just popped out." Jenny exulted. "I didn't even know I was going to say it!"

"Kensington." My finger found the listing. "There's a Kensington Avenue downtown. There's a Kensington Street in Kirkland and a Kensington Circle in Roxborough."

"We'll hit them all." Larry snatched the book from my hand. "Come on, Jen."

"Wait!" I called after them. "How do you know Kensington wasn't her New York address?"

"Because I know she lived on West Sixty-first Street in New York," Larry shouted back.

The door slammed on his last word and it wasn't until his silly little car shot backward down the driveway that I thought to ask about my money from the game table.

Dismantling the cabinet took an hour. There were six drawers with exquisitely carved fronts and brass pulls, one of which was missing. I called Rena and made an appointment with her to either match or replace the pulls, then put a load of the endless laundry into the washer. Jenny's sores were fading and she was no longer scratching but I was reluctant to stop the routine until Dan checked her.

I was preparing supper when they returned, downcast.

"The Kensington in Kirkland is a day nursery." Larry was despondent. "The Roxborough one is a retired couple. They were nice, they let us try the key. It didn't fit. The downtown Kensington is a hole in the ground."

"A what?"

"An excavation. You know, board fence all around, the crane in the middle, something going *gadoom-gadoom*? The guy said they're putting up an office building."

"Maybe the key was for whatever was there before they dug the hole. Did you ask anybody?"

The phone rang before he could answer. It was Mike.

"Does Jenny remember the name of the hospital she was in?" he asked.

I relayed the question. Jenny shook her head.

"No. But from what she told us, I think it had to be in town somewhere. St. Mary's? The Jewish General?"

"One or the other. Okay."

"Mike?" I said sharply, afraid he would hang up. "Have you found anything? Any answers?"

"Yeah. Some. There's a couple more people I want to talk to. I'll know more then. Look, Cat, I'm in a guy's private office and I've gotta get off his phone. I'll come by in the morning. Okay?" He hung up.

We ate in the living room, watching Jenny be beautifully evil—or evilly beautiful, whichever—in "Halls of Justice." After three hours of depressingly predictable dialogue through which the plotline crawled a centimeter forward, I was bored, Jenny exhausted. Larry decided to go home.

"I'll be back in the morning," he said. "If Mike gets here before I do don't let him start without me."

12

Okay." Mike pushed his coffee mug aside. He retrieved a file folder propped against the leg of his chair. "This is what we know for sure." He opened the folder, his eye on Jenny. "Does the name Jason Cody ring any bells?"

Jenny frowned, shaking her head. "No."

"He was killed—bludgeoned and stabbed repeatedly—in your apartment last year. November eighth."

The terse statement shocked us. Larry's arm froze, his cup halfway to his lips. He lowered it to the table. "What apartment?" he asked.

Mike picked up a sheet of paper from the folder, a photocopy of a newspaper clipping. "This is what the newspapers had," he said. "You can read it later."

"What apartment?" Larry insisted. "Where?"

"Kensington." Mike's glance dropped to the photocopy. "Eleven-seventy Kensington Avenue."

Larry frowned. His gaze flicked from Mike to Jenny and back. "We went there today," he said. "Eleven-seventy's a hole in the ground."

"It is now." Mike nodded. "A year ago it was a house, an old brownstone." He closed the folder. "Why don't I tell it the way I got it. Cat? Any coffee left?"

"I'll make fresh." I couldn't resist adding, "You're drinking too much coffee."

"Yes, Mother." Mike raised suffering eyes to the ceiling.

I put coffee on to perc and returned to the table.

"When I found the story in the newspaper morgue," Mike began, "I called an old friend, Harry Stone. He's a police captain now. He put me together with Al Rosen, the homicide detective who worked the case. Al was cooperative, a nice guy. He let me have what he had."

Mike took a pen from his pocket and rolled it with his fingers, a substitute for the cigarette he still craved. He squinted at Jenny.

"It seems you were living with this Jason Cody in New York. You told Rosen you came here because a friend of yours was sick and Cody came with you. He had some business to take care of, photography you assumed, you weren't sure. Cody was a commercial photographer, evidently pretty good."

Mike turned his gaze on Larry.

"The brownstone on Kensington, the owner, a Mrs. Aldred, lived on the ground floor. The upstairs had been rented as a furnished apartment. Jenny'd had the lease on it for almost seven years."

"Seven years!" Larry shot a glance at Jenny. "You kept an apartment here? Even while you were in L.A.? In New York?"

Jenny spread empty hands, a helpless gesture.

"For whatever reason, the apartment was yours." Mike looked at Jenny. Her face was chalky.

"It's okay, kid," he said, his voice gentle. "You didn't have anything to do with Cody's death. You weren't even there when it happened. Do you want to hear the rest of it?"

"Yes."

"According to the autopsy, he suffered a heavy blow to the head, at the back here." Mike tapped the base of his skull. "But that isn't what killed him. There were eight stab wounds in his body. He was stabbed with a kitchen knife. He bled to death."

Mike paused. "You okay?" he asked Jenny.

Jenny nodded mutely.

"Good girl." Mike smiled at her. "Okay. When Cody was killed you were at the hospital with your agent and an actress named Sherry Miles."

"Jenny was with Hannah?" I asked.

Mike nodded. "Hannah Peel. She'd had a stroke. Sherry Miles drove Jenny home from the hospital. Jenny invited her

in for coffee, they walked in on the bloody mess together."
Mike raised his brows at me. "Speaking of coffee . . . ?"

"Hannah died of a stroke?" I brought the carafe to the table
and filled Mike's cup.

"Eight days later. A second massive stroke."

Larry shifted impatiently in his chair. He waited till I sat
down. "Go on, Mike," he said. "So the guy was dead . . ."

Mike nodded. "Cody was killed on the eighth while Jenny
was visiting Hannah at the hospital. On the ninth Jenny was at
the hospital again. She stayed until ten in the evening. She left,
telling Hannah she'd be back the next day. She never showed.
Al was working a heavy caseload and it was a couple of days
before he got back to Jenny. By then she'd vanished. Al meant
to try again but there's somebody getting themselves shot or
stabbed or strangled every day. The Jason Cody case was put
on the back burner. Filed and forgotten."

"And Jenny, too," Larry said.

"As far as Al was concerned, yes." Mike reached for the
carafe, refilled his cup. "When I told him the rest of the story
he did some digging. There were two hit-and-runs that night,
the ninth of November. An old man and a young woman. The
old man in the east end, the young woman on Trenholme,
about halfway between the Jewish General and Kensington
Avenue. A man named Hollis Porter called the police. I went
to talk to him."

Mike frowned. He looked at Jenny, his expression uneasy,
then at me. "This is where it starts to get weird," he said.

"Starts? What's it been so far?"

"Okay. Weirder." Mike drank off his lukewarm coffee,
grimaced, and set the cup aside.

"First of all, this Hollis Porter is an engineer, a very precise
guy, mid-fifties, I'd guess. He lives on Trenholme. He was
walking his dog that night, November ninth, as he said he
does every night, between ten-thirty and eleven. He'd just
started out, got halfway down the block, and saw a girl coming toward him, walking at a good clip, he says. Biffy, his dog,
wagged his tail and whuffed at her as they came together. The
girl stopped and let the pooch sniff her boots. She patted the

dog, smiled at Porter, said 'Nice dog', and carried on."

Mike nodded at Jenny.

"Porter got a good look at you. Long blond hair, light eyes. He guessed blue. Five-eight he figured. Slim. Said he thought he'd seen you before but couldn't say where or when. He said he'd know you if he saw you again."

"He'd seen her on TV," Larry said.

"Probably. Anyway, Jenny headed up the street, he headed down. Porter says he'd only taken a few steps when Biffy decided he'd found the perfect spot to take a dump. Porter was standing against a cedar hedge, waiting, and he saw a car coming down the street, same direction the girl'd come from. He said he wouldn't have particularly noticed except it was running without lights and coming very slowly. He said for some reason he looked to see where the girl was, he didn't know why. She'd reached the corner and had just stepped off the curb to cross the street. The car was alongside Porter by then. Porter said the headlights came on and the car roared forward. He yelled something, he doesn't remember what. The girl turned, the car hit her, and then it took off like a bat out of hell down Trenholme."

Jenny made an odd, grunting sound in her throat.

"Was it a red car? Did he say?" she asked.

"He said maroon. Burgundy? Maroon?" Mike bent toward her, eyes narrowed. "Why? Do you remember a red car?"

Jenny shook her head. "It's a car in a recurring dream. I'm out under a bright light somewhere and a red car is coming at me. It doesn't hit me. The hood opens like a huge mouth and bites my arm off."

Mike snorted, grinning, and she giggled. "I know. It sounds funny. But believe me, in my dream, it is *not* funny."

"I'll tell you something else that isn't funny," Mike said. "If that car had come at you the night before, you'd be dead meat. Porter says the car bounced you off your feet into a pile of garbage bags filled with dead leaves. He said if the tenth hadn't been a garbage collection day you'd have sailed head first into a fieldstone wall. He also said the police pissed him off royally. They persisted in calling it a hit-and-run; he insisted it was deliberate, no question. He's positive that car was out to run you down."

Jenny was shaken. "Why would anybody want to kill me?"

"Why would anybody want to kill Jason Cody?" Mike picked up the newspaper photocopy and read aloud. "Headline: *New York photographer murdered.* News photographer Jason Cody, was found stabbed to death in an apartment at eleven-seventy Kensington Avenue. The body was discovered last night by his live-in companion, actress Jennifer Steele, when she returned from visiting a friend at Jewish General Hospital. Police state Cody had been dead for at least four hours and are investigating the possibility of an interrupted burglary."

"Burglary?" Jenny frowned.

Mike flipped the paper aside. "Standard cop handout," he said. "But there were no signs of forced entry. Nothing was missing. And eight stab wounds? Rosen thinks Cody was killed by someone he knew."

"Did he have any idea why?"

"Any number of reasons. He could have been a threat to somebody. Possibly revenge, who knows? There's a lot of rage in eight stab wounds."

For a moment we silently envisioned the savagery of a knife, thrust eight times into living flesh.

"Mike," I said. "Do you think Cody's killer was the same person who tried to run Jenny down?"

"Could've been. Who knows? If we ever find out why Cody was killed . . ." He shrugged.

"What do you think?" I persisted.

"What do I think." Mike leaned back, folded his arms across his chest, and eyed us, one after the other. "Okay. Let's try this on for size. Cody comes here on business, according to what Jenny told Rosen. Cody's a photographer. Let's say, for the sake of this scenario, he has photos of somebody doing something they shouldn't be doing? Let's suppose his business here is blackmail."

He paused, tilted his head at me. "How'm I doing so far?"

"Come on, Mike," I said impatiently. "Get on with it."

"Hey, Cat," he protested, "I spent half the night working this out, pushing the pieces around, making them fit. You're getting the condensed version. Indulge me."

I raised my hands.

Mike nodded. "So Cody contacts the blackmailee, his victim, the guy he's planning to blackmail. Let's call him Mack the Knife. Cody makes an appointment with Mack. He specifies a time when he's sure Jenny won't be home. Mack comes to the apartment. He kills Cody, takes the photos, and leaves, figuring that's the end of it, he's home safe."

Mike unfolded his arms, picked up the newspaper story.

"Next day he finds out Cody isn't alone. There's a girlfriend in the wings. Does she know about him? Is she in on the deal? Mack figures he can't take the risk."

Mike tapped the photocopy. "It's all here. Who she is. He might even have seen her on television, can recognize her. He parks outside the Jewish General, waits for her, not sure how he's going to do it. He gets lucky. She comes out alone, starts walking. He tails her and gets his chance when she steps off the curb to cross the street. He guns the motor, hits her, and takes off in a cloud of heifer shit and small pebbles. She's dead and his troubles are over."

"Except she's not dead," Larry said.

"*Ahah!* But he doesn't know that, does he? He watches the papers, checks out TV, the *Halls of Justice* soap. Jennifer Steele has vanished off the planet. And time marches on."

"And he's gotten away with murder," Larry said.

"Right." Mike nodded. "So far. So let's move right along to act two."

"Act two? What's act two?"

"Act two opens with Jenny regaining her memory. She goes back to work, resumes her career. And one day old Mack turns on his TV and gets one hell of a shock. Jennifer Steele, the woman he killed, lives! End of act two."

"Is there an act three?" Jenny unexpectedly spoke up.

Mike looked at her. He hesitated, then answered. "I don't know. I haven't figured it out yet."

"You think he'll come after me again, don't you, Mike?"

Jenny said quietly. "That's act three, isn't it?"

Mike pushed back his chair and stood up. He stretched, smiling down at Jenny. "Relax, Jen. Everything I've said is pure speculation. Mack the Knife is a fictional character and bears no resemblance to anyone, living or dead."

"But it all fits."

"It only fits what we know at this point. What we don't know could change the entire plotline. You just take it easy, kiddo. Get healthy, get well. There is no act three."

He put his hand on my shoulder. "Gotta go, Cat. See you, kids. Larry. Jen."

I pushed away from the table and walked with him to the front door. "Come back for supper if you like," I said.

He shook his head. "Thanks, Cat. But if it doesn't inconvenience you, I'd really like to come tomorrow."

"So come tomorrow. Why? What's tomorrow?"

He dipped his head, abashed. "It's my birthday."

"Well, happy birthday. I'll make something special. What would you like?"

"Potato pancakes," he said promptly.

"Done."

"And Cat," he added, his expression sober. "Tell Jenny to forget it. The whole thing, what I rambled on about, is pure horse pucky. And don't you worry either, okay?"

"I won't," I assured him.

But watching him drive away I knew I would. As Jenny had said, it all fit.

13

Marcie called early.

"Dan wants to see Jenny today," she said. "I have an opening at three-thirty."

"Three-thirty?" I hesitated. I was to meet with Rena at three.

"Is that a problem?" Marcie asked.

"Uh. Sort of. I have an appointment at three."

"Catherine," Marcie said, her voice dry. "It isn't you Dan wants to see. Put Jenny in a cab." She hung up.

The doorbell buzzed as I replaced the receiver. Feeling put upon, I went to answer. It was Larry.

"Larry," I said. "Don't bother to ring. Just walk in from now on, okay?"

"Sure. Thanks," he said cheerfully, trailing me to the kitchen. He set a brown paper bag on the counter. "Scones and bitter orange marmalade," he announced. "Plus," he said, reaching into his pocket, "your money from Irving. Forgot to give it to you yesterday. Sorry."

"Thank you. Did he give you a hard time?"

"He tried. You do a lot of work for him?"

"Not a lot. And I don't think I'll be doing any more."

"Good. The man's a one-cell animal."

"Who's a one-cell animal?" Jenny asked from the doorway. She came into the kitchen tying her robe.

"Hey, Jenny." Larry's face brightened. "Irving. Bottom of the food chain. How're you feeling?"

"I'm fine," Jenny said absently. She looked at me, her face clouded. "I've been thinking about what Mike told us. Do you think he's right?"

"Right? You mean right about the facts? Or right about what he called his scenario?"

"Both, I guess."

"About the facts, you can bank on it."

I put the scones into the toaster oven to warm, poured three mugs of coffee, carried them to the table.

"Mike's a writer, Jenny," I continued, "which means he has a typical writer's quirk. He'll start with bare bones and build a hypothetical superstructure over them. Half a dozen if he likes. And all of them will fit the facts. The scenario he gave us was simply game playing. Conjectural exercise. It was never intended to be taken literally."

Jenny's face cleared. I breathed a silent sigh of relief. She, at any rate, was reassured.

"I have a couple of problems." I changed the subject quickly. "Dan wants to see you at three-thirty. I'm meeting with Rena at three and she lives way across town."

"So I'll take Jenny to see Dan," Larry said. "Next?"

"That cabinet in the living room. It has to be carted down to the basement, to my workroom."

"Consider it done," Larry said.

Rena had neither a matching drawer pull for the cabinet nor suitable replacements.

"Leave me the one you brought with you," she said. "I'll check on Sunday at the flea market. Sam might have something. If he doesn't, I'll look around on Friday."

"Old Sam or Young Sam?" I asked.

"Old Sam. Young Sam has moved to Seattle."

We sat in Rena's cluttered kitchen, drank herbal tea, and gossiped about the denizens of the weird and wonderful world of flea markets.

When you're in it—as I was when I sold off the pack-rat accumulation of three generations who had inhabited the house I bought—you are almost instantly absorbed into a subculture possessed of its own customs and characters, a milieu less and less peculiar as you become familiar with other vendors, most by face, many by first name, some by the name given them by others.

The nicknames can be devastatingly accurate and are universally recognized by vendors who move from one flea market to another throughout the week. Everyone knows that Shifty George, a Hungarian of dubious honesty who considers lewdly offensive remarks made to any woman over the age of fifty to be a form of gallantry, is not Saint George, a prissy Bible-thumping Brit who specializes in sterling silver and royalty memorabilia.

Rena and I had shared a booth at two of the flea markets I did that year. We had worked the long, tiring days together and become friends. She was an experienced vendor who viewed the world passing by her stall with a jaundiced eye. We now met rarely, always without strain.

I left when the old brass ship's clock on her kitchen wall clanged four bells. On the way home I picked up a Black Forest cake and arrived home seconds before Mike swooped into the driveway, driving heavy-footed as always, and screeched to a halt less than two feet from where I stood.

"One of these days, Mike." I shook my head.

"At any speed, under any conditions, and no matter what you happen to think," Mike retorted, "I am always in complete control of my vehicle."

It's a threadbare argument, not worth pursuing.

"Okay, Sterling Moss." I handed him the big white bakery box. "You take the cake."

"Very funny."

"It's your birthday cake, idiot. Happy birthday."

"Black Forest?"

"What else?"

He followed me into the house, his limp more pronounced than normal.

"Your leg bothering you?"

He grimaced. "Goddamn prosthesis rubs on a rash I picked up in Hawaii." He swung the box by the string. "Where d'you want me to put this thing?"

"Anywhere. Put it anywhere. Put it on the dishwasher."

I bent to get the sack of potatoes from beneath the sink and heard a crash, a shattering of glass, an explosive *"Holy shit!"* from Mike.

Chunks and shards and crumbs of black glass littered the floor. Jenny's vase had shattered into a million pieces.

"What happened?" I asked stupidly.

"I don't know." Mike's voice rose. "Jesus Christ! Scared the shit out of me! I didn't even see the goddamn thing! What the hell was it?"

"Jenny's vase."

"Oh, shit." He bent and scrabbled at some larger pieces. *"Shit.* What the hell was the goddamn thing doing on the goddamn dishwasher anyway?"

"Mike! You'll cut yourself. Wait. I'll get the broom." I reached into the closet behind me. "It was on the dishwasher because I hoped it would help her remember."

"She'll remember all right. She'll remember some asshole named Mike smashed her goddamn vase because some damn fool named Cat left it on the goddamn dishwasher."

"Mike! For Pete's sake! What's done is done! It wasn't a priceless antique. It was a black glass vase."

Mike straightened, peered down at a black lump in his hand. "This isn't glass," he said. "This is wax. And there's something stuck in it."

"What? What do you mean?"

"Give me a knife."

I handed him a knife from the drawer. He began carving at the lump in his hand. Black shreds peeled away and fell to the countertop.

"What is it?" I leaned forward to see.

"Black wax. Stuck around something." A glint of gold appeared. "There." Mike dug into the wax and detached a small slab. "It looks like a key. A brass key of some kind."

While I swept the floor, Mike held the key under the tap, letting the hot water melt away the residual wax.

It was a strange-looking key, approximately three inches in length, two-thirds a hollow brass tube, the balance a flat oval disk embossed with a dragon's head.

"I've seen one like this before." Mike frowned. "Years ago. It came with an Oriental chest Meg had. I wonder how long it's been stuck in that vase."

"Could be anywhere up to sixty years. The vase was an art deco black amethyst glass piece from the thirties."

"Was it valuable?"

"Twenty, maybe thirty bucks." I gathered the ingredients for potato pancakes. "Maybe less. The only real value it had was that it seemed important to Jenny. We don't know why."

"Shit," Mike said. "She's going to hate me."

"She won't hate you, Mike. Accidents happen. I'm sure she'll understand. Come on, tell me about Hawaii. There must have been something nice about it."

Mike sat down at the table, his face glum.

"Well, Haleakala, one of the mountains on the island of Maui, was pretty impressive," he admitted, and proceeded to ramble on about pumice beds, cinder cones, lava tubes, and sulfur banks, typically Mike. I listened, more or less, peeling and grating potatoes and onions, adding eggs, flour, and bread crumbs. I formed the pancakes on the hot griddle, left them to fry, and joined him at the table.

Mike stopped in mid-phrase. He sniffed the air.

"That smell." He beamed. "Oh my, that glorious smell. Takes me right back to when I was a kid. *Pliatski*, we called them in Ukrainian. *Pliatski i smetana*. Maddy made them at least once a week, the best *pliatski* in the world. In the universe. God, how I loved them."

"They were Laurie's favorite, too." I smiled to myself at the memory. "I think they're the only things she ever learned to make. She hated cooking. Everything took too long for her. If you couldn't microwave it, she wasn't interested."

I stopped abruptly. Mike's face had assumed a gentle, patient expression. He would listen as long as I chose to talk, retelling Laurie, repeating Laurie stories he had heard before, probably more than once. Displeased with myself, I went to turn the pancakes.

A car door slammed outside. I heard the front door open and close. Jenny and Larry were home.

"Laurie!"

I looked up, startled.

Jenny stood in the kitchen doorway, her eyes enormous. Two bright spots of color burned on her pale cheeks.

"Laurie," she cried. *"I remember Laurie!"*

14

$\mathcal{T}\!\mathit{he}$ minute I walked in the door!" Jenny marvelled. "It was as simple as stepping from one room into another! No trumpets. No blinding flash. It was just all there!"

She bent low over the griddle, sniffing. "The smell of potato pancakes! That's what did it! Do you believe it? Laurie and potato pancakes. Remember the time she grated her thumb, Catherine? Blood all over the place? Remember what she said? *Okay, so what, so we eat pink pancakes?* How old were we? Fifteen? I remember it was the year we made the volleyball team. Remember? Laurie couldn't . . . ."

She stopped abruptly. "God. Listen to me. I'm babbling like an idiot," she said. "There's so much swirling around in my brain my head feels as if it's going to burst."

"Before you blow away, you want to take a look at this?" Mike showed her the brass key. "Does it mean anything to you?"

Jenny took the key from Mike's outstretched hand. "Where did you get this?" She frowned.

"It was in that vase of yours. I'm sorry. I broke the damn thing. I'll try to replace it. I'm really sorry, Jen."

"Forget it, Mike. Please. It was an ugly old thing. I kept it because it belonged to my mother, but I never liked it much." She dismissed the vase impatiently. "How do you mean, it was in the vase? I never saw it there. Did you, Catherine?"

I shook my head. Mike answered.

"It was embedded in a ball of black wax melted down into the bottom of the vase. Somebody went to a lot of trouble to put it there. We wondered who. Also why and when."

"Jason." Jenny turned the key in her hand. "It's the key to a lacquer box he picked up in Hong Kong. He kept expensive lenses in it. Negatives. Papers. Personal stuff."

"Negatives?" Mike jumped on the word. "D'you know what they were?"

"Not really." Jenny's nose wrinkled. "Porno, probably. He once showed me photos he'd taken of some senator, I've forgotten which one, some southern state. Disgusting stuff. I thought they were sick. He thought they were funny."

Mike nodded. "Figures," he said thoughtfully. "I wonder what happened to that box."

Jenny shrugged. "He brought it with him, I know that for sure. He never went anywhere without it. I suppose it's floating out in space somewhere, along with all my stuff."

I jumped to my feet.

"Charlie!" I exclaimed to three startled faces. "Charlie told me the vase came in an estate sale job lot." I went to the phone and began dialing. "Could be the box was included. Describe it, Jen. Quickly."

Jenny frowned at the ceiling. "About the size of a bread box, but half as deep. Black lacquer. Brass binding. There's a mother of pearl medallion on the lid. The handle's a brass dragon and it locks with a funny-looking brass padlock."

"Good girl."

Charlie picked up on the fourth ring.

"Hi, Charlie, it's me, Catherine. Listen, the estate sale where you got the black amethyst vase Jenny was after? You don't happen to remember if there was a black lacquer box with a brass dragon handle?"

"Matter of fact, I do," Charlie said. "Very nice. Not old but nice. It was locked. No key. Why?"

"Is it anywhere you can get at it quickly?"

"I imagine it's down in the storage room somewhere. I'd have to look. Why? Is it important?"

"Mike thinks a man named Jason Cody was killed because of what's in it."

"Mike? Mike Melnyk? Is he back?"

"He's here. It's his birthday."

"Hey. Wish him happy birthday for us."

I relayed the message. Mike nodded impatiently. "Ask him

if we can come and get the box," he said.

"I heard that," Charlie said. "Does he mean now?"

"Now?" I asked Mike. He nodded. "He says yes. Now."

"Hold on." I heard Charlie's voice, muffled through his hand, distant words from Rafe. "Cat? We're going to an auction tonight, out in your general direction. We'll drop it off on the way."

"That would be great. Thanks, Charlie."

"*Nada*. See you in an hour or so."

I replaced the receiver. "They're bringing the box."

"Good." Mike nodded, satisfied. "So when do we eat?"

I set out the salad, pancakes, and sour cream, formed six more pancakes on the griddle, and sat down.

Mike spooned sour cream onto his pancakes. "Tell me something, Jenny. Why would this guy Jason go to so much trouble with the wax? Who was he hiding the key from?"

"Me," Jenny said.

"You?" Mike's brows rose. "Why would he have to hide it from you?"

"He began hiding the key after I flushed his stash down the john," Jenny said.

"What stash?"

"Coke. Cocaine. About six-hundred bucks worth. He got even by cutting half my wardrobe into two-inch squares. Took him an entire day."

"Cute," I said. "Jenny? Did you ever . . . ?"

"No way. Never. Not after I found Miss Tiddleywinks OD'd on the dressing room floor."

"Miss Tiddleywinks?"

"The one before me. She was twenty-two years old and she was stone-cold dead. I'd just done some voice-overs for the station. I was there, so they fast shoved me in front of the camera and told me to 'tiddley.' I shook like a leaf the entire half hour."

"Migod. That's how you became Miss Tiddleywinks?"

"Right over her dead body," Jenny said with a note of sour flippancy in her voice. "Didn't even miss a beat: She's gone, you're on. I was so turned off I wouldn't even touch an aspirin after that. It drove Jason up a wall. I couldn't drink and I wouldn't snort." She smiled at Larry. "Real partypooper, me."

"What was he like?" Larry grinned back at her.

"Jase?" She tilted her head. "Tall. Well-built. Auburn hair and the bluest eyes this side of Paul Newman. Loads of wild Irish charm. And a mean streak a mile wide. We were in the process of breaking up when Hannah had a stroke."

"Why did he come here with you?" Mike asked.

"Money. He was always broke."

"Money? Did he say from where?"

"No." Jenny frowned. "Actually, he didn't decide to come till the last minute. I used to pick up the Sunday *Gazette* at an out-of-town newstand. He'd glanced through it and got all excited about something and said he was coming with me."

"He didn't tell you why?"

"Only that somebody owed him money. A lot of money."

I got up from the table and went to turn the pancakes. "Just out of curiosity," I said, "why did you maintain an apartment here?"

"Until *Halls of Justice*, I was back and forth a lot. A couple of weeks in L.A., a week in New York, a week here, that sort of thing," Jenny explained. "It wasn't exactly an apartment, actually. It was just the master bedroom on the second floor of an old brownstone, converted. There was a bathroom and a built-in kitchenette, but mostly it was this big room, with a gas fireplace. And Mrs. Aldred, my landlady, was a sweetie. Hannah thought I should hang onto it until I was established somewhere."

"What about the New York apartment?" Larry asked. "I read in some soap opera rag that you lived on West Sixty-first Street."

"I did. But it wasn't my apartment. It belonged to an actress on location in Spain. Hannah arranged for me to live there until she came back. Six months." Jenny's face clouded. She frowned down at her empty plate. "Hannah. What am I going to do without Hannah?"

"How come your agent was this Hannah person?" Mike

asked. "If you were working in New York and Hollywood, how come your agent was here?"

"Hannah wasn't just an *agent*," Jenny said. "She was a den mother to her talent. We all kept in touch with her. I had a Hollywood agent for a while, but we didn't really click. Then I got *Halls of Justice* and Hannah started lining up Matt Steiner, a New York agent, for me. Then she . . . the stroke."

Jenny bent her head, her fingers at her forehead, hiding her face. "God, I'll miss her. I'll never stop missing her."

We had nothing to offer but a sympathetic silence.

I served the pancakes. While we ate, Mike launched into an acidly funny description of a luau under the stars, complete with pig and poi, obese and gray-haired tourists wearing plastic leis mutilating the hula, and musicians wearing plastic smiles, strumming Hollywood-inspired island tunes on plastic ukeleles.

Rafe and Charlie arrived as I was clearing away the cake plates. Rafe's eyes widened when he looked at Jenny but he said nothing.

"Happy birthday, Mike. Good to see you." Charlie set the lacquer box on the table. "Nice piece. Too bad it's new. You have the key?"

"Jenny has it," I said. "Rafe? You don't normally buy this sort of thing. How come?"

"It came with an estate sale on Kensington a couple of months ago," Rafe said. "The old lady died and her son sold us the house contents, all or nothing."

Jenny silently handed the key to Mike.

"That black vase you were after," Rafe continued, "and this box were in a carton we found in the basement, stuck away in a corner with a couple of other cartons and some suitcases. They're still in the storage room at the shop, along with all the junk from the house we've been too busy to go through and heave out."

Mike gave a sudden grunt of triumph. He unhooked the oddly shaped padlock and threw the box lid back.

The first thing we saw were three glassine envelopes filled with white powder.

"Uh-oh." Mike tossed them to Jenny. "What d'you want to do with these?"

Jenny flicked the envelopes away.

"Okay," Mike said. "Down the loo. Let's see what else we have here."

He removed five small leather boxes, checked each before setting it aside on the table.

"Lenses." He brought out a cardboard folder and peered inside. "Negatives. We can go through them later." He reached into the box and brought out a white envelope with *Acapulco* scrawled across it, opened the flap, and withdrew a thin pack of photographs.

"*Bingo,*" he said softly.

There were fourteen photographs, in lurid color, of five men, past middle age, performing sexual acts on one another and on three dark-eyed, black-haired boys who looked to be no more than ten years old.

Mike peered at the top photo. "Holy Nellie," he said. "Julian Shaw."

Charlie reached for the photo. "Who is Julian Shaw?"

"He's a municipal court judge. Sonovagun."

At the third photo, Charlie laughed. "Morley," he said, and handed the snap to Rafe. Rafe nodded.

"Who's Morley?" Mike asked.

"Morley Richards. A customer of ours. He collects art deco."

Morley Richards was the most attractive of the five men, if men in bestial poses performing obscene acts can be called attractive at all. He was well-built, sandy-haired.

"Look at the bastard." Charlie marvelled. "He's had more face-lifts than Phyllis Diller. The guy's pushing sixty-five and he could pass for forty."

Julian Shaw, obese and hairless, looked porcine beside a man whose body was matted with dark hair. The fourth man, chubby, bald, and wearing heavy horn-rimmed glasses, bore a startling resemblance to an uncle of mine, long dead. The fifth man matched my mental image of Cervantes's Don Quixote, lean, swarthy, and saturnine.

"You said something about somebody being killed because of what was in the box," Charlie said. "What was that all about?"

Mike explained. He laid out his scenario. When he finished, Charlie shook his head.

"You can rule out Morley," he said. "There's no way this guy Cody would get a dime out of him. Morley's the man who carries the banner at gay activist demonstrations."

"Okay. So that leaves four others. Julian Shaw and three men we can't identify."

"Morley would know who they are," I volunteered.

Charlie nodded. "And we'll probably see him tonight at the auction." He glanced at his watch. "If we leave now we can catch him before the auction begins."

"Do you think he'll tell you anything?"

"Morley? Sure. He'll think it's a real hoot."

"Take the pictures with you," Mike said. "And while you're at it, ask him if he knows how Jason got them. Ask him if Jason was there."

Charlie and Rafe left, promising to call after talking to Morley. Mike reached into the box again.

"Let's see what else we have here," he said.

There was a yellowing birth certificate, a five-by-seven blue envelope, and a passport.

"Cute fella." Mike flipped through the passport. "Looks like he got around a lot, too."

He handed the well-worn passport folder to me. The harsh photo showed a redheaded man, handsome in a boyish way. I passed it on to Larry.

"This'll give you a giggle." Mike slid the birth certificate across the table. "Jay Cee, our Jason Cody, was born in Bethlehem. How about that? Bethlehem, New Hampshire. Twenty-nine years ago."

He picked up the blue envelope, removed a paper, and unfolded it. "Marriage license." He looked across at Jenny. "Did you know he'd been married?"

"Married?" Jenny took the certificate and frowned at it.

"Montpelier, Vermont. Jason Francis Cody. Nancy Lee Rountree. Eight years ago? He'd have been just a kid eight years ago."

"Twenty-one. Big enough and old enough," Mike said. "He never told you?"

"No." Jenny folded the paper and handed it back to Mike. "Catherine? Do you think Charlie and Rafe would mind if I went through the stuff left from Kensington? Some of it might be mine. The suitcases. Maybe my clothes?"

"I'm sure they wouldn't mind. I'll ask Charlie. He said he'd call after he talked to Morley. I'll ask him."

"Would you ask him if tomorrow would be okay?"

"Sure."

"Thanks." Jenny pushed herself to her feet. "Would anybody be mad if I went to bed?" she asked. Her voice was husky with fatigue. "I'm totally burnt."

"You're entitled." I smiled at her. "Go ahead."

"G'night, then. Happy birthday, Mike."

"Thanks, kid. Go to bed."

She started from the room. At the door to the hall she paused, turned.

"Where's Laurie now, Catherine?" she asked. "Did she marry that nice man she was seeing? What was his name? Andy?"

"Andy. Yes, she married Andy." *And they're living on a sunny Greek island and she's painting Aegean seascapes and he's writing a book about the ancient Mycenaean civilization.* "They died in an automobile accident. Last year."

Jenny's eyed widened and filled with sudden tears. They overflowed and spilled down her pale cheeks. She made a soft, whimpering sound, turned, and fled down the hall.

"Rough," Mike said gruffly. "Wake up and find everybody you know is dead."

"Should I. . . ?" Larry half rose from his chair.

I shook my head. "I don't think so, Larry. I think she's going to have to work it out on her own."

Larry stood up. He stretched tiredly. "I guess I'll go home

then. I'll come back in the morning. If Charlie says it's all right, and if Jenny wants to go tomorrow, would you tell her I'll take her down to the shop?"

"Of course."

"I'll see you in the morning, then." He touched Mike's shoulder as he passed. "Happy birthday, Mike."

"Thanks." Mike nodded. "Goodnight, Larry." When we heard the front door close, he added, "Good kid."

"Especially for Jenny."

"How about some coffee?" Mike took the cardboard folder from the lacquer box. "I'll go through these negatives, see what's in them, before we put a match to them. You agree we should burn them?"

I went to the sink and filled the percolator. "Either burn them or flush them with the cocaine. I don't want any of that slime in my house."

"Yeah." Mike peered up at a strip of negatives he held to the ceiling light. "Pretty sick stuff."

"Those old men, I don't care." I scooped coffee grounds into the top of the percolator. "They can screw whatever they like—turtles, elephants, or a pound of liver. But those boys, those three little boys . . ." I slammed the percolator top into the base.

"That's odd." Mike's voice was puzzled. "The negatives aren't here. There's some pretty scruffy stuff, but not the negatives of that particular orgy. Strange."

The phone rang before I could comment. It was Charlie.

"I've only got a minute before the auction begins," he said, "so listen."

"I understand. Go."

"Morley said the pictures had to have been taken two years ago. He said Julian Shaw was in Spain last year from August until Christmas. You can eliminate Shaw."

"What about Morley? Do we eliminate him?"

"Cat, forget Morley," Charlie snapped. "I'll fill you in later. Just listen, okay?"

"Sorry."

"The one with the horn-rimmed glasses is an art dealer

from San Francisco, Paul Tobias. The hairy one is René Junot, owns a restaurant in New Orleans. The skinny, dark man is Raúl DeSoto. He lives in Acapulco. It's his house. Morley says Cody wasn't there, at least Morley didn't see him. But he says Raúl could have hired Jason to stay out of sight and take pictures, it's the asinine sort of thing Raúl would do to amuse himself. I gave Morley the photos. That's it. Okay?"

"Wait! Charlie! Can Jenny come down and go through the Kensington stuff tomorrow?"

"Sure. Anytime." He hung up.

I replaced the receiver and repeated the conversation to Mike. He listened, frowning.

"Well," he shrugged, "I guess that blows my theory right out of the water. Jason was after somebody here, not in San Francisco or New Orleans." He chuckled suddenly. "Shifty little bastard, wasn't he? He must have run off a set of prints before he turned the negatives over to this DeSoto character. I wonder how vulnerable those other two men are."

"The ones in San Francisco and New Orleans? Who cares?" I lifted the drained percolator top, set it in the sink.

"*Cat!*"

The word was a strangled cry. The hair on the back of my neck lifted. I swung around.

Mike was bent forward in his chair, a fist pressed to his throat. His eyes were wide with fright, his face ashen.

15

The price is too high."

"What?" I was driving too fast to risk more than a quick glance at Mike, huddled in the passenger seat beside me.

"The price is too high. Ninety-five cents worth of pain for every five cents worth of joy. It's a lousy deal."

"Mike." I raced a yellow light to the corner, shot through the intersection on the red. I slowed down, shaken. "Don't try to talk. Just hang on. We're almost there."

"There's an elephant sitting on my chest. My heart's bouncing around like a ping-pong ball. I'm scared shitless. I've gotta talk. Talk to me, Cat, for God's sake."

"Okay. Okay." *Talk about what?* "Tell me about the five cents worth."

"The five-cents worth? The joy?" He was breathing heavily, the words came slowly. "It used to be Meg. It used to be my job, getting my teeth into a good story. Getting it first and getting it right. It used to be Nick."

He fell silent.

"And now?" I prompted.

"Now?" He gave a rusty chuckle. "Now it's a good crap. Yeah, and knowing most of the people I made a fool of myself in front of are either senile or dead."

"Dammit, Mike." The hospital lights were half a block ahead. I pressed down on the accelerator. "Don't make jokes."

"Who's joking?"

I sped past the hospital's main entrance, came to a screeching halt at the emergency doors, helped Mike from the car, pushed through into a crowded waiting room, and clutched at the sleeve of a passing, white-coated young man.

"Heart. His heart," I panted. "Can you help me? It's his heart."

He shook my hand loose, glanced at Mike's blanched face, and said, "Stand here. I'll be right back."

He returned seconds later, pushing a wheelchair.

"Get in," he said brusquely.

Mike sat, darting a beseeching look at me.

"I'll park the car," I began, and raised my voice as he was wheeled away, "and come back."

An hour later I was permitted into a six-bed ward where Mike, third bed to the left, lay on his back, eyes closed, looking wan against the crisp white hospital linen.

A clear plastic tube rose from his nostrils to an outlet in the wall behind his head. Two black wires that led from a black box suspended from the ceiling, disappeared down the neck of his pale green nightgown. Taped to his arm was a needle, fed by a plastic tube leading to a bag of colorless fluid hung from a contraption beside the bed. His prosthesis had been removed and lay, fleshly pink and somehow obscene, on the sill of the deep-set window.

The plastic-upholstered chair beside the bed *whuffed* softly as I sat down. Mike's eyes flew open, found me.

"Hey, Cat," he said weakly.

"How're you feeling?" I took his hand in mine. It felt hot and dry.

"Lousy," he whispered huskily. He cleared his throat. "I feel like a punctured balloon."

"Then don't talk. Go to sleep. I'll stay here."

He squeezed my hand. His eyelids fluttered closed. Soon, the cramped tension lines melted from his face, his breathing regulated, and he slept.

The room was quiet. I slowly became aware of low-key sounds; a soft hiss, labored breathing, a barely audible keening, the faint, spasmodic ponging of a call bell, a distant, metallic voice mouthing unintelligible words.

I looked around. Heavy breathing came from the next bed, its occupant hidden behind a drawn curtain. In the bed across a black-bearded man lay, spread-eagled, both hands heavily bandaged, a turban of bandages sheathing his right eye and his hair.

Mike stirred. I released his hand and sat back, thinking about him and his ninety-five cents worth of pain.

Too many painful losses. His wife, Meg, killed in a car bombing aimed at another man, a mistake that had also cost him a leg. Maddy, the sister who had raised him, her husband, and son, all gone. And Nick, the foster son he had loved, *still* loved, lost to a life he could not countenance.

We met a year ago, when my life was in turmoil. I was in over my head in a dangerous situation and he helped extricate me. When the dust settled we found we were friends.

It was an easy, relaxed relationship. When he ran into a brick wall in the book he was writing; an encyclopedia of organized crime, local and statewide; he called. When the smell of stripper and stain became too oppressive, I called.

We met for dinner three of four times a month. If we ate out, it was on Mike. At home was on me. Occasionally, we took leisurely country drives, with me at the wheel. Mike was too lead-footed for my peace of mind. We would talk or not, our silences were comfortable.

When the holidays came, a difficult time for both of us, we spent Christmas day serving turkey dinners at a downtown mission that Mike supported. New Year's Eve we ignored.

I smiled to myself, remembering my birthday.

We were in a French restaurant of Mike's choosing. My birthday cake, a Gateau Saint-Honoré, had just been served, together with coffee and liqueurs.

Mike sipped his Cointreau, wished me happy birthday, and said, "You want me to make a pass at you?"

"What?" I looked up from my slice of that delicious cake, totally startled.

"Kind of dates me, doesn't it." Mike frowned. "What's the current propositional phrase? Come onto you? Want me to come onto you?"

"I understood the pass bit." I set my fork down. "What I don't understand is, what brought this on?"

Mike indicated the restaurant with his liqueur glass.

"Last time I was in this place was . . ." His brows lifted. "Migod, it was twelve years ago. I brought a lady friend here to celebrate her promotion. She'd been made copy chief or creative director or whatever. Anyway, the coffee comes and she asks me why I've never made a pass at her. Don't I find her attractive? I don't remember what I said, probably something stupid. I sure as hell couldn't tell her the truth, that she reminded me of that broad in *Network*, remember that movie? We were never really easy with each other after that and we just sort of drifted off in different directions."

I reached for my Cointreau, sipped, and set the glass down. Mike watched, his expression unreadable.

"Do you find me attractive?" I asked.

"You?" He was obviously taken aback. "Of course I find you attractive. You're a very attractive lady."

"Good. So let's not spoil a beautiful friendship." I picked up my fork. "At this stage of my life, I don't need all that grief. The misunderstandings. The hurt feelings. I don't need the faking. And all that dressing and undressing? I don't want a lover. I want a friend."

"Good." Mike was grinning broadly. "So if I just happen to feel like putting my arm around you, you won't think I'm trying to jump your bones."

"Jump my bones?" I laughed at a sudden memory evoked by the words. "You know the last time I heard that? It was on the dumbest, most tasteless television show I've ever seen. Ten people, not one of them under seventy, all simpering and twittering about their fabulous sex lives. A silly grandmaw, who should have known better, giggling that her boyfriend, this scrawny rooster she's got a hammerlock on, can't wait to jump her bones. And the old boy grinning a store-bought smile and looking as if he wouldn't have the strength to jump to a conclusion. It was pathetic. Maybe it was meant to be sweet. Or humorous. It came off as embarrassing."

"What was the name of the show?"

"God, I don't remember. 'As The Stomach Turns'?"

Mike laughed. "Let me tell you about embarrassing and pathetic," he said. He finished his Cointreau and gestured to the waiter for another.

"It was a couple of years after I got the prosthesis," he began. "She was a very pleasant woman, a widow. I didn't know her all that well, she was a friend of a friend, that sort of thing. Anyway, she was going to be my first try at, uh, fabulous sex, after I got the peg leg."

The waiter set a new glass of Cointreau on the table. Mike nodded his thanks, waited for the waiter to move away, and continued.

"They tell you more than you'll ever want to know about your damn prosthesis. However, they do not tell you the protocol involved in, uh, fabulous sex. I mean, do you take it off or leave it on? And if you take it off, when? Before you start fooling around? I mean, pardon me, while I take off my leg? Or do you take time out after things get steamed up? Who the hell are you going to ask? You're strictly on your own out there."

"What did you do?"

"When the clothes came off, the leg came off. I figured maybe that was the least awkward move?"

"Problem solved?"

"Yeah. *That* problem. But with two elbows and only one knee, you've sort of got another problem. You're a three-legged table, not all that well balanced. I hinted it might be a good idea if she got on top but she wasn't having any of that perverse stuff. She made it clear it was to be the old missionary position or forget it. Well, hell, I figured, if I put my mind to it? The trouble was, as soon as it began to get interesting, I'd lose my concentration. I'd start listing sideways and have to go back to square one. Then, all of a sudden, it got very interesting and I forgot everything but *wheee!* Fabulous sex! Except my balance was kaput. I fell off her. I not only fell off *her*, I fell off the goddamn *bed*, down onto the goddamn floor. Knocked the wind out of me. When I got my breath back, I started to laugh."

"What did *she* do?"

"She was not amused. And it didn't help that I couldn't

stop. There I am, hopping around on one leg, my limp dingle-dangle swinging in the breeze, and I've got a galloping case of the giggles. She dressed, fast, and left, fast. I called her the next day to explain. Or apologize, whatever. She hung up on me. I don't blame her, I guess. What the hell, we wouldn't have made it anyway."

I must have dozed. A light touch on my shoulder brought me fully awake.

"Mrs. Melnyk?" A matronly nurse bent over me. "You may as well go home. He'll sleep through the night. There's nothing you can do here. Why don't you go home?"

"Can I come back in the morning?"

She nodded. "Family members are permitted to visit any time after eight o'clock."

I drove home through the midnight streets, past darkened suburban houses where young families slept. We get too soon old, I thought. We live in the now, thinking it's forever, and suddenly now is yesterday and the world has moved on.

Dammit, Mike. Don't die on me. Who else do I know who remembers Zasu Pitts?

The house was as we'd left it, lights blazing, an acrid smell of coffee, long overheated. The envelopes of cocaine and the negatives were still on the kitchen table.

While I unplugged the percolator, poured the coffee down the sink, cut up the negatives, and flushed the pieces down the toilet together with the cocaine, I debated whether to call Nick, Mike's estranged foster son. I knew Mike could not accept Nick's shadowy connection with organized crime. At the same time, I was aware of the indissoluble bond of affection between them.

Finally, I went to the kitchen and dialed the phone number of the Capri restaurant.

A man answered on the third ring. I asked to speak to Nick Kramer.

"Mr. Kramer is not here tonight," an accented male voice informed me.

"Can you tell me where I can get in touch with him?"

"Ah. A moment, please." I listened to background music and a hum of conversation, then the man returned, read out a number. "You try him there, please."

This time I reached an answering machine, Nick's voice saying, "Leave your name. I'll get back to you."

"It's Catherine Wilde, Nick. Mike's had a heart attack. He's at Lakeshore General. I'm going back at eight o'clock tomorrow morning. If you call, call before then. Good-bye."

I replaced the phone, locked the doors, turned off the lights, and went to bed.

16

In the morning I was dressed by seven-forty-five. I was writing a note to leave for Jenny, when the doorbell rang. I went to answer, mildly annoyed at Larry for not simply walking in, as I had invited him to do.

Nick Kramer stood on the stoop, his hand raised to ring once more.

He was thinner than when I'd seen him last, a little more than a year ago. His black hair, longer then, was cut very short. But his eyes, thickly lashed, vividly green, and beautiful, were the same.

"Good morning, Catherine," he said.

"Come in, Nick." I stepped aside. "I expected you to phone. I'm just getting ready to leave."

"I thought I'd go to the hospital with you. If you don't mind." He followed me to the kitchen. "How's Mike?"

"He was sleeping when I left last night." I bent over the table, finishing the note for Jenny. "I haven't called the hospital this morning. Did you?"

He didn't answer. Suddenly the air I was breathing seemed thicker, heavier. In the quivering silence I was aware of the refrigerator's hum, the clock's measured ticking. I looked up, filled with an atavistic sense of alarm.

Nick's eyes, as focused and intense as those of a cat waiting out a motionless bird, were fixed on the doorway to the kitchen, where Jenny stood, impaled by that green gaze.

In her rumpled, oversized T-shirt, her hair tousled from sleep, she looked as defenseless as a child. Her eyes had darkened to a cobalt blue. A bright spot of color burned on each cheek. Her pale lips were parted in confusion.

I crumpled the unfinished note. "I'm glad you're up, Jenny.

This is Nick Kramer. Nick, Jenny Steele. We're going to the hospital, Jen. Mike's had a heart attack."

Jenny drew in a ragged breath and blinked. The taut wire vibrating between blue eyes and green snapped.

"A heart attack?" She turned to me. "Mike?" she asked, her voice shaken. "When?"

"After you went to bed. I took him to Lakeshore General last night. We're going down there now."

"Wait. I'll get dressed. I'll go with you."

I shook my head. "Larry's coming to take you down to Canterbury House. To go through the Kensington boxes. Charlie said you could come anytime."

Jenny turned and, without speaking, walked away. Nick's eyes followed her down the hall. The bedroom door closed firmly.

"Was it something I said?" he asked, amused.

"Nick. You didn't say anything." *The hell you didn't,* I thought. *You said plenty, but not with words.* "Let's go. Your car or mine?"

"I'll follow you there. I can't stay long."

Mike was sitting, fully dressed, in the plastic chair I had occupied the night before, working the crossword puzzle from the morning paper. He looked up, capped his pen, and grinned at our astonished faces.

"Some heart attack," Nick said drily.

Mike stood up. "Paroxysmal tachycardia. No big deal."

Nick frowned. "No big deal? What the hell is paroxysmal tachycardia?"

"Your heart speeds up to a hundred and sixty-something beats per minute. Scares the shit out of you but it isn't fatal. Not even serious. Just leaves you feeling as if you've run the marathon. The doc says I'll take a pill every day, no problem." He waved the subject away. "You're looking skinny, Nick. You all right?"

"I'm fine. Dammit, Mike, you scared me. Let's get out of here."

"I'm waiting for the doc's final okay and some papers I

have to sign. I was going to phone Cat to come pick me up."
He looked at me. "How's Jenny doing?"

"She seems to be coping. Why?"

"Because I've been thinking, ever since they woke me up at
some ungodly hour this morning, and the way I figure it is
this—if it isn't the dirty old men, it has to be the marriage
license."

"Now there's a provocative lead line." Nick was amused.
"Dirty old men? Marriage license? What's the story, Mike?"

Mike raised his eyebrows at me.

"You tell him," I said.

Mike talked and Nick listened; Mike with the clarity and
precision of the good newspaper reporter he had been, Nick
with the somehow menacing stillness and total concentration
I had seen in him once before.

Mike paced, recounting everything from the day I first saw
Jenny. Nick perched on the windowsill, legs outstretched and
crossed at the ankles, his arms folded over his chest, his head
lowered.

"Okay," Mike concluded. "We found the marriage license
in the box. But no divorce papers. Now, for argument's sake,
let's suppose there never was a divorce. And suppose further
that the bride . . ."

"Nancy Lee Rountree." I supplied the name.

". . . whatever. Suppose . . ."

"What did you say?" Nick's head had reared up. He over-
rode Mike's words.

Mike and I exchanged glances, startled at the sharp reaction, uncertain which of us he was questioning.

"What did you say her name was?" Nick asked.

"You mean Nancy Lee Rountree?"

"You're sure that was it?" Nick pressed.

"I thought it had a nice lilt to it," I said. "Nancy Leeee
Roundtreeee. Sure, I'm sure."

Nick looked at me, then at Mike. "You don't know who
Nancy Lee Rountree is?"

I shrugged. Mike spread his hands. "Should we?" he said.

"Ever hear of Hamilton Bradford Manville?"

Mike's eyes narrowed at Nick. "Money. Lots of it. Didn't he die a couple of years ago?"

"The old man did. Nancy Lee married the son, Ham Junior. Nancy Lee Rountree is Mrs. Hamilton Bradford Manville the second."

"The society bimbo? You sure?"

Nick nodded. "I know her."

"You don't happen to know her well enough to ask her if she bothered to divorce Jason Cody before she married Ham Junior, do you? Ham, Jesus what a name."

"I'm sure she did."

"But if she didn't?"

"I can possibly find out."

"How?"

"I'm a lawyer. Remember?"

"Oh, yeah. Right. For some reason I keep forgetting you went to law school."

"Pop. Don't start." Nick glanced at his watch. "I have to get moving. Look, I mean it, if you want to drop the marriage license off at my office, we can try to track down the divorce papers."

"If they exist."

"If they exist. But I think you're reaching."

"So indulge me."

Nick's face softened. "Sure. Take care, Pop."

"Yeah. You, too."

"Always. So long, Catherine. Thanks for calling."

An hour later, after Mike had signed more papers than I had when I purchased my house, we were on our way home.

"Pull up at the next drugstore, would you, Cat?" Mike said. "I'll get this prescription filled before I lose the damn thing."

The curb in front of the next drugstore was lined with parked cars. I let Mike out and circled the block. He was outside, waiting, on my third go-round. He ducked around a double-parked van and climbed into the passenger seat.

I smelled the smoke before I saw it curling up from Mike's cupped hand.

"Aw, Mike. No."

"Leave it alone, Cat."

"Four months. You've gone four whole months."

"Cat . . ."

"But you've gone through the worst of it."

"The worst? Tell me about it." Mike yanked the ashtray out from the dashboard and stubbed his cigarette butt. "In four months I've written fourteen pages. Four-fucking-teen pages. You know what I do? I sit at that damn computer and think about how much I want a cigarette. Okay? Plus I just blew a month and a shitload of money on a trip I didn't want and sure as hell didn't enjoy, because a stop-smoking expert said a change of scenery works wonders."

"You haven't given it time, Mike. You can't undo forty years in four months. It's a habit. It's an addiction."

"Goddammit, Cat, I know it's a habit. I know it's an addiction. I also know that, outside of getting my leg blown off, I've never had a sick day in my life. So I quit smoking and what happens? I have a heart attack."

"You said tachycardia wasn't a heart attack."

"It bloody well felt like one. And I bloody well thought it was one—they run in the family. I'm lying there, wired up like a toaster, and I'm thinking, hell, I'm sixty-two years old, I could die tomorrow, and the only regret I'd have is for the last four months of unproductive misery. So screw it. I'm going to enjoy my one remaining vice."

"There's nothing I can do to stop you?"

"Not unless you can one-hundred-percent guarantee I'll get younger and prettier."

"Huh."

We drove the rest of the way home in silence. I parked beside Mike's car and asked him if he wanted to come in for coffee. He shook his head.

"I want to go down to the *Gazette* to check something."

"Check what?"

"Jenny said Jason hadn't intended coming with her until he saw something in the Sunday *Gazette* that made him change his mind. I want to go back to that Sunday *Gazette* and see if I can spot anything significant." He climbed out of my car.

"Cat? Would you get the marriage license for me? I'll drop it off at Nick's office while I'm downtown."

He was in his car, with the motor running, when I came back.

I handed the marriage certificate through the open window. "Do you really think this thing means anything?"

"I don't know. But it's a loose end. And I don't like loose ends."

"Once a reporter, always a reporter?"

"There's that. There's also the fact that whoever killed Jason Cody must have thought he had a damn good reason to go after Jenny. We can't assume he won't try again when Jennifer Steele is resurrected."

"Act three? I thought you said there was no act three."

"I lied."

17

Jenny and Larry returned with two cardboard boxes, a large blue suitcase, a smaller, matching overnight case, and a dark green nylon duffle bag.

"We had to break the locks." Larry set the suitcase down in the middle of the kitchen floor. "The keys must have got lost in the shuffle somewhere."

"And we found my purse in the suitcase!" Jenny dangled a black leather handbag by the shoulder strap, swinging it like a pendulum. Her face was luminous.

"Your purse? How did it get in the suitcase? Didn't you have it with you when you went to the hospital?"

Jenny shook her head. "I never took it with me when I walked. Especially in New York. I'd just put some money and my key in my pocket." She dumped the contents of the purse on the table. "IDs, address book. And credit cards. *Yay!*"

"What's in the boxes?"

"Books, junk from way back. I didn't go through them. Most of my clothes are in the suitcase. The duffle bag is—was—Jason's."

"I checked the duffle bag out," Larry said. "I thought there might be an address book, notes, something? Nothing. Just clothing, some his, some Jenny's. Whoever packed just crammed it all in—his, hers, whatever."

"Uh." I looked at the bags and boxes occupying the center of my kitchen. "Why don't you two sort this stuff. I've got about an hour's work in the basement. Then I'll do something about dinner."

Jenny looked up from the red address book she was riffling through.

"Forget doing dinner," she said. "We're going out. On me. Let's find out if any of these credit cards are still operative."

Our waiter, a slender Taiwanese with an unshakeable smile, placed the tab beside Larry's plate. Larry picked it up and handed it back to him.

"Give it to my sister." He grinned across the table at Jenny. "She's paying."

Jenny dropped her Visa card on the tray the young man held and watched his receding back.

"If it's good, I'll use it tomorrow." Her voice rasped, a sure indication she was tiring. "I'm going to New York."

"New York?" Larry's head reared up. He set the pot of green tea back down on the table without refilling his cup. "You're going to New York tomorrow?"

"If I can get a flight." Jenny's lips thinned at the faint echo of disapproval in Larry's words. Larry recognized the warning sign and turned to me, his eyes appealing for support.

"You don't think you're rushing it a bit?" I stepped in cautiously. "Maybe you should check with Dan first?"

"I don't need to check with Dan. I'm fine."

"What did he say the other day? I forgot to ask."

"He said take the pills, rest when I get tired, eat properly, come back in a week. He said I'm doing fine."

"Even so. Your energy level still drops like a stone. Why not wait awhile? New York isn't going anywhere. Why the urgency?"

"Why the urgency?" Jenny's hands tightened into fists. "For one thing, I need an agent. I need to find out if Matt Steiner is still interested. For another, I left everything I own in Carmen's apartment, including my checkbook. All my money is in New York. I need that money. I can't mooch on you and Larry forever. I need to go. I need to get my life back."

The outburst drained her. She propped her elbows on the table, dropped her head in her hands.

"Damn." She dug her fingers into her hair. "I'm pooped.

But I'm going, dammit. Even if I have to crawl around town on my hands and knees, I'm going."

Larry's face melted. He reached across the table and placed his hand over hers. "Okay, tiger," he said. "If you've gotta go, you've gotta go. But I'm going with you. There's no way you're crawling around New York on your own."

As Jenny's head lifted, the waiter appeared at her side, tray in hand.

"Sorry, please," he said. His smile was relentless. "Not good. Visa say not good."

Jenny's cheeks flushed scarlet. I lifted her credit card from the tray and replaced it with three twenties. The waiter shot a dark glance at Jenny and hurried away.

Dejected, Jenny dropped the offending card into her purse. "Maybe I should try Mastercard tomorrow . . ."

"Forget MasterCard tomorrow," Larry said. "I've got enough plastic to fly us to the moon."

"I can give you the money when we get there."

"Or we can put it on your tab."

"That tab of mine is going out of sight."

"Who's counting?"

Larry dropped us off at home.

"It's only nine o'clock," he said. "I might as well drive out to the airport and pick up the tickets tonight."

"Not too early a flight," I said.

"Anything after noon, okay? I'll make hotel reservations while I'm at it. Any particular hotel, Jen?"

Jenny, leaning wearily against the car, shrugged.

"Any suggestions, Cat?"

"I used to like the Doral. It's small and quiet. But that was years ago. I don't know if it's still there."

"So, small and quiet, right?" His head tilted on his slender neck and I had a sudden image of a bird, head aslant, probing the meaning behind human sounds.

I couldn't help laughing. "That wasn't a dictum, Larry. That was nostalgia for my misspent youth."

He eyed me uncertainly. "Oh. Well. So, I'll call you in the morning. Okay?"

"Perfect." I smiled at him across the generation gap. I slipped my hand through Jenny's arm and drew her back from the car. "Goodnight, Larry."

The phone began ringing as I closed the door behind us. I turned to the right, bound for the kitchen; Jenny drifted left, on her way to bed.

"Where the hell have you been?" Mike demanded before I could say hello. "I've been calling for the last three hours."

"We went out for dinner . . ."

"When are you going to get rid of that goddamn antique and get an answering machine?"

I looked down at my old black rotary dial phone. I liked it. "Jenny got her things back . . ."

"Or get a call display. I wouldn't have to keep calling back to make sure I get you."

"They're going to New York tomorrow."

"What? Who?"

"Jenny and Larry. Why were you calling? What's wrong?"

"What are they going to New York for?"

"So Jenny can get her life back." I decided to leave it at that. I could fill in the details later. "Mike? How about we go back to square one. You've been calling for three hours. For what?"

"I wanted to make sure you weren't planning anything for tomorrow afternoon."

"What's happening tomorrow afternoon?"

"Hang on a minute. I'll get a cigarette."

The wire hummed while I thought about the times I most missed smoking. Talking on the phone. With breakfast. After dinner. What the hell, most of the time.

"Okay. I'm back." Mike paused and I could picture him, lighting up, inhaling . . .

"I checked out the Sunday *Gazette* for the weekend before Jenny came back with Jason," Mike said. "November sixth, last year. There was a picture of the Children's Wish Foundation ball patrons on the society page. Guess who's in it."

"Nancy Lee."

"Nancy Lee, hubby Ham, and momma-in-law Caroline. Among others. Jason couldn't have missed it."

"Mike? You don't think you might be reaching? It's hard to imagine . . ."

"Let me finish," Mike interrupted. "I went to see Nick, gave him the marriage license. He said he didn't guarantee anything. It would be proving a negative. By the way, he asked a hell of a lot of questions about Jenny. What happened there?"

"Nothing happened. Unless you consider thunderbolts and steamy air a happening."

"No kidding." Mike chuckled. "Nick? Jenny? I wouldn't have thought she was his type. That explains it, though."

"Explains what?"

"Nick called me later, at home. Told me he'd set me up with someone who could answer any questions I had about Nancy Lee Rountree Manville. Three o'clock tomorrow. He suggested I take you with me."

"Take me where?"

"To see Dr. Rosemary Chang. She's a child psychologist. She's also Nancy Lee's sister."

18

I drove Jenny and Larry to the airport. Larry was reluctant to leave his car in the parking lot for an extended period.

"It'll be gone by tomorrow morning," he said. "Mercedes are number one on the hit list."

So the kiddy car was a Mercedes?

Jenny's energies had been restored by twelve hours of undisturbed sleep. She moved with a new, brisk confidence.

Her subtle makeup had been expertly applied. Gold hoops dangled from her earlobes. Her lustrous, red-gold hair was deceptively casual. She wore a shockingly expensive suede suit in a wildly flattering shade of sage green, purchased by Larry on his way to the house this morning. On her feet were copper-toned lizard pumps, rescued from the blue suitcase. A small, matching handbag hung from her shoulder on a narrow gilt chain. She was perfect. She was Amanda Prentiss, *Halls of Justice* beauty.

She was Jennifer Steele. I wondered how I had ever thought her plain.

She leaned into the car window. "I'll call you tonight, Catherine," she said.

"Have you got your pills?"

"All of them."

"Don't forget to take them."

"I won't." She withdrew from the window and turned to take her small case from Larry.

"Jenny?" I leaned across the passenger seat to call to her. "Good luck!"

She flashed a wide smile and blew me a kiss, the first theatrical gesture I had seen her make since the day I found her at Canterbury House. I drove down the loading ramp to the access road, my mind alive with an intriguing realization.

I don't even know Jennifer Steele.

I had known Jenny, Laurie's teenage friend, more or less superficially, as any working mother knows her child's peers. I had known the eager-young-actress-Jenny, mainly professionally, back in the days when I helped launch her career. All more than ten years ago. And those ten years in the show-business jungle, as much as anything before, had gone toward the molding of an unknown—to me—quantity named Jennifer Steele.

She had lain dormant for a year inside the filthy bag lady, had stirred in the sickly waif I had brought home.

Now she's awake and a stranger.

I smiled to myself. It's the first question we ask about celebrities. What's Elizabeth Taylor really like? What's Bill Clinton, Tom Cruise, Princess Di—what are they really like?

What is Jennifer Steele really like?

I had three minutes to change before Mike would arrive. I stripped off the jeans and sweatshirt I wore and put on my old standby, the Liz Claiborne suit I had paid twenty-five dollars for at a garage sale five years ago. The lines are classic, the fabric, a pink raw silk, is timeless. Most important, I'm comfortable in it. I hate new clothes. You never know how they're going to behave.

Mike nodded approval and headed toward his car. I dug in my heels.

"No way, Mike. I drive or I don't go."

He grunted, limped to my car, and climbed into the passenger seat.

I started the car. "Where are we going?"

"Roxborough." Mike reached into his pocket, pulled out a pack of cigarettes, and began the search for matches. "Chang lives in Roxborough. Her office is in her house."

"Use the dash lighter. Where in Roxborough?"

"Cherry Lane. Fourteen Cherry Lane. Do you know where Cherry Lane is?"

"I think so." I backed out of the driveway, into the street, and drove to a red light at the corner. "Tell me something. Why am I going?"

"Nick suggested . . . hell, Nick insisted you go with me."

Startled, I glanced at Mike. "He did? Why?"

Mike grinned. "He's under the mistaken impression that you're a gentling influence on me."

"Hah." The light flashed green. I crossed the boulevard and fell in with the traffic flow. "Why do you want to talk to this woman? What do you expect to get from her?"

The dash lighter popped. Mike removed it. He lit his cigarette, inhaled. "I want as much information as I can get about Nancy Lee."

"Nancy Lee is her sister. What makes you think she'll tell you anything?"

Mike exhaled irritably. "I don't know that she'll tell me diddly-squat, Cat. She's a place to start, that's all. Pick enough scabs, you're going to get blood."

"Talk about messy metaphors. What are you going to do? Tell her you think her sister is a murderer? Murderess?"

"I'm not going to tell her anything."

"Why don't you go to the police? Your friend, Al. . . ?"

"Rosen. Al Rosen. With what? A marriage license? The Manvilles are prominent people. The police aren't about to mess with them, Cat. They'd need a lot more than a marriage license and a few unfounded suspicions dreamed up by a has-been newspaper reporter to take on the Manvilles. A hell of a lot more."

We entered the town of Roxborough. I concentrated on finding Cherry Lane, a street I dimly remembered as parallel to Commercial Center Street.

"There it is ahead." Mike leaned forward, pointing. He turned his head to me. "Cat? Let me do the talking, okay?"

"Gladly."

Fourteen Cherry Lane was a sprawling white-brick ranch house set behind a well-tended lawn and a rock garden abloom with asters and marigolds.

The driveway, wide enough to accommodate two cars, led

to a section of the house that must, in the original plans, have been intended as a double garage. In place of garage doors was a bay window, framed in stained oak, and a dark oak-panelled door.

A polished brass plaque invited us to please ring, then enter. Mike pressed the brass button embedded in the door frame beneath it.

We stepped into a waiting room, panelled in honeyed pine and furnished in maple colonial. A lit driftwood lamp added its soft glow to the sunlight filtering through the leaves and fronds of the many plants that filled the bay window recess on our left.

Above a beige tweed couch on our right was a framed hooked rug, an autumn scene worked in faded colors. On the cobbler's bench in front of the couch, a copper bowl held a riot of fresh orange marigolds.

As I was appreciating the calculated serenity of the room, a door opposite us opened and a woman emerged.

She was tall, five-nine or -ten, and the dark gray suit she wore was designed to disguise the extra weight she carried. Her straight brown hair was unstyled, cut short. Her face, bare of makeup, was plain, nose too long, chin too short, mouth too generous. But her doe-shaped eyes were beautiful. Large, darkly fringed, the whites pearlescent, the irises warm brown velvet.

"Mr. Melnyk?" Her voice was low-pitched. "I'm Rosemary Chang. Come in, please." She stepped back and we followed her into an office that was an extension of the waiting room.

She circled a large pine desk and seated herself behind it, her back to a bay window glassed to the floor.

"Please." She gestured at two chairs opposite her.

Mike held the chair for me. "This is Mrs. Wilde, Doctor Chang," he said. "Mrs. Catherine Wilde. A friend."

She flicked a glance at me, nodded, then silently watched Mike seat himself.

Mike's hand strayed to his pocket. "Do you mind if I smoke?" he asked.

"I mind," she replied.

For a moment there was a faintly antagonistic silence. I wondered which of them would break it. Rosemary Chang blinked first.

"I understand you'd like to ask me some questions about my sister. About Mrs. Manville."

"Not so much ask questions," Mike said. "I imagine you know her better than most. Maybe you could just sort of talk about your sister, give us an idea of what she's like?"

She looked at him expressionlessly, and I wondered what Nick had told her, what sort of pressure had induced her to submit to this invasion of her privacy.

She swivelled her chair a quarter of a turn and focused her gaze on the trees beyond the window. "Nancy Lee," she said. "She's a Gemini. She's twenty-eight years old. Married. No children. Have you ever seen her?"

"Only in pictures." Mike spoke to her profile.

Doctor Chang nodded. "Then you know she's beautiful. She was a beautiful child. She's a beautiful woman. She's a talented artist. Or could be. She plays the piano, not well. She rides well. Loves horses, always has. She's an expert skier, an indifferent cook."

Rosemary Chang tilted her head back. "Let's see," she mused, staring at the ceiling. "As Mrs. Manville, she devotes a great deal of time to charity work. She donates a day a week to the Sick Children's Hospital. This year, she's honorary chairwoman of the Kidney Foundation. She is also actively engaged in raising funds for the Caroline Manville Retreat House for Battered Women. I don't think she's doing anything about AIDS yet, but I'm sure she'll get around to it sooner or later."

Mike looked at me with startled eyes. I shrugged.

When it became obvious nothing more was forthcoming, Mike leaned forward.

"Tell me, Doctor Chang," he said, "was Nancy Lee married before? Before she became Mrs. Hamilton Manville?"

It was Rosemary Chang's turn to be taken aback. She abandoned her contemplation of the ceiling and swivelled to face us. "Married before? Nancy Lee? No. Never."

"You're sure? You would know if she had?"

"Don't be ridiculous," Chang snapped. "She's my sister. Of course I'd know."

Mike's eyes narrowed at her tone but he remained calm.

"What kind of car does she drive?" he asked. "What color would it be?"

"I don't know one car from another. But the color would have to be white."

"Oh?"

"Everything Nancy Lee owns is either white, black, or beige. Everything. Her clothes. Nancy Lee never wears any color but white or black or beige. It's her trademark."

"Trademark?"

"So the society pages say."

"I see." Mike waited, then asked, in a dead level tone I recognized as a danger signal, "Isn't there any insight you can give us into your sister? How she thinks? What sort of person she is?"

Rosemary Chang shrugged, her face closed. Seconds ticked by, then Mike stood up abruptly.

"Then thanks for nothing, lady," he said. "You haven't given me anything any idiot reading the social pages doesn't already know. You and your friend Kramer are about as useful as tits on a bull. Come on, Cat, we're out of here."

We were halfway across the waiting room before she called out to us.

"Wait!"

Mike turned. I followed him back to the office. He faced Chang across the desk, his face impassive.

"How well do you know Nick Kramer?" she asked.

Mike's brows lifted but he said nothing.

"Do you know what he is?"

Mike shrugged. "I know he's a lawyer."

"He's a gangster, Mr. Melnyk. I worked for him. I know who his clients are and I know exactly what they are. I know of his association with Carmine Diano and I know who and what Carmine Diano is. A mob boss. A don. A godfather. All those cutesy things. Naturally, I wonder about you, Mr. Melnyk."

"Oh, naturally, of course. What did Kramer tell you?"

"Nothing. Just to give you any help I can."

"Got you scared, has he, Doc?" Mike's grin was evil.

"Scared?" Chang's voice was cold. "No. I'm not afraid of Nick Kramer. I owe him. I owe him a lot."

There was a gleam of satisfaction in her eyes at the surprise on Mike's face. She looked at me. There must have been something in my face she liked, something she could connect with. She relaxed.

"I went to work for Nick when I was eighteen," she said. "I was taking night courses at the university, three nights a week." She smiled at me. "I've wanted to work with children all my life."

I returned her smile.

"On school nights, I'd bring my supper to work," she continued. "I'd stay in the office, eat, and study until it was time to go to class. One night—I'd been there almost two years—Nick asked me why I was always around after everyone else had gone home. I told him. He's very easy to talk to. He has that way of really listening, you know?"

I nodded. It's the eyes, I could have told her, and the stillness. They cast a spell.

"He called me into his office next morning. He told me I was fired, that I was to go to school full-time. My tuition and living expenses would be taken care of until I graduated. I remember the absolute surge of joy I felt. I would graduate in two years, not six. But I told him it was impossible for me to accept an education financed by dirty money. I'm sure I sounded insufferable, but I did mean it."

She stopped and smiled down at her hands, clasped before her on the desk. "I expected him to throw me out on my ear," she said. "He didn't. He simply said the money would come from a fund that had nothing to do with his business. Clean money. He called it *meddis* money. *Mattes* money? Some name that sounded like that."

"Maddy's money!" I exclaimed. "Maddy Svarich! She was a schoolteacher. She financed Nick's education." I glanced at Mike for feedback, got none. "She was Mr. Melnyk's sister."

Chang's head snapped up. Her wide eyes flicked from me to Mike. She pushed her chair back, stood, and moved to the bay window, her back to us.

Oh hell, I thought, *I've blown it.* I looked at Mike, prepared for flashing daggers. He winked at me.

We waited a full minute before Rosemary Chang turned to face us. She directed those lovely eyes at Mike.

"What is it you want to know, Mr. Melnyk?"

"Mike."

"Mike. What is it you want to know?"

"Anything you can tell us that will help us understand what sort of person your sister is."

She nodded. "I see. Would you excuse me for a moment? I'll be right back."

She left the room through a door leading to the house proper and reappeared almost immediately, carrying a large framed photograph. She gave it to Mike, returned to her chair behind the desk, and sat down.

Mike glanced at it and passed it to me.

It was a color portrait of a family—father, mother, two daughters—posed against a misty studio backdrop.

Rosemary, looking only slightly younger than she did now, stood beside a slender man, shorter than she, whose facial features she shared. His right arm circled her waist, his left hand lay on the shoulder of his wife, seated in front of him.

She was a big woman, big-boned. Standing, she would have been as tall as Rosemary, taller than her husband. Her blond hair had been teased into a smooth round ball surrounding a face too wide for the small, pert nose, the rosebud mouth. Her eyes were her commanding feature; large, perfect ovals, the irises a remarkable shade of turquoise.

Seated beside her, hands clasped in a white froth of organdy on her lap, was the prettiest young girl I've ever seen. Her hair was white-blond, her eyes vivid turquoise, her nose perfectly sculpted, her mouth pink and moist. She held her slim, immature body erect, her head poised on a long, slender neck.

"Nancy Lee is four years younger than I am," Rosemary said. "I was seventeen when that picture was taken. Nancy Lee was thirteen."

"She's very pretty." I handed the picture to Rosemary. She placed it, facedown, on her desk. "Fascinating eyes. The color."

"Quincy eyes. They run in the family. My mother was a Quincy, you know."

I didn't know. Mike evidently did. He nodded.

"My father . . ." Rosemary hesitated, then resumed. A harsher note crept into her modulated voice. "My father died shortly after that picture was taken. We were in a private school, Nancy Lee and I, when he died. We finished the year, of course, fees are always paid in advance, but college was out of the question for me. I took a computer course and went to work for Nick Kramer. Nancy Lee was placed in a school for gifted underachievers."

"Gifted underachievers?" The phrase, used in that context, was new to me.

"A euphemism for bone-lazy brats with high IQs," Mike provided. Rosemary permitted herself a small smile. "So Nancy Lee has a high IQ."

"Yes." Rosemary leaned back in her chair, her eyes on Mike. "Do you know what an egocentric personality is?"

"I know what the word egocentric means."

Rosemary nodded. "Egocentrics' interests are limited to their own activities, to satisfying their own needs. Only the area immediately surrounding themselves is real to them. The rest is empty space. Other people come alive solely in that area. Other people don't exist, other than in that area, and they exist there only to service the egocentric. Essentially, to the classic egocentric, a washing machine and a hairdresser are of equal substance and value. The one launders her clothes, the other her hair."

Mike's eyes narrowed. "What is it you're telling us? That your sister, that Nancy Lee, is an egocentric?"

"To the max." The slang term, coming from Rosemary's mouth, sounded strange. "The frightening thing is, there's no malice in Nancy Lee, even a sort of innocence."

"Why do you say frightening?" I asked, intrigued. "If there's no malice . . ."

"Because there's no sense of evil. Since she lacks any conscience and feeling for others she can be unconscionably destructive in her pursuit of gratification. When she was a child and lied to avoid punishment, usually diverting the blame to me, she was unable to comprehend my anger. She had explained to me why she had to lie. Didn't I understand?" Rosemary's mouth pursed. "I hated her when we were children."

"And now?" Mike asked.

Rosemary shrugged. "I've no reason to hate her now. We never see each other."

"You don't?"

Rosemary's face darkened. When she spoke there was the residue of a hundred old resentments burning deep under the anger in her voice.

"James, my husband, is a dermatologist," she said. "Shortly after we were married, Nancy Lee went to see him about having a mole removed from her buttock. James came home that night and told me flatly that if I wanted to see my sister I could meet her for lunch or wherever I chose but she was no longer welcome in our home. Of course I asked why. It seems Nancy Lee had been coming on to James for more than a year. That day she had gone too far. She'd made a crude pass in front of his office staff. James had thrown her, *literally thrown* her, out."

There was a sudden gleam of amusement in Rosemary's pretty eyes. "She landed square on her butt out in the hall," she said. "I wish I'd seen it."

The glimmer vanished. "She didn't deny any of it when I confronted her. She explained she had always wondered about Chinese men. The point is, she didn't understand, she truly *did not understand*, why I was so hurt and enraged. She didn't understand how James could have behaved so brutally toward her. She'd only been curious. Were they different in bed? I haven't seen or spoken to her since."

We sat in silence for a moment, then Mike said, smiling, "I thought you said she was smart."

Rosemary surprised me by smiling back at him.

"When Nancy Lee was twenty-four," she said, "she decided she was going to be the next Diane Sawyer. I assume you know who Diane Sawyer is?"

Mike nodded.

"She prepared a script, talked a well-known civil rights lawyer into doing an interview with her, took the tape to a television station, and convinced them they needed her."

"They hired her?" There was surprise in Mike's voice.

"They hired her. Believe me, Nancy Lee, with all pistons pumping, is very hard to deny. She lasted three days."

"They fired her." Satisfaction replaced surprise.

"On the contrary. They offered her the moon."

"She was good?"

"Better than good. Her ideas were imaginative. She was painstakingly thorough in her preparation. Her diction was flawless. The camera loved her. The only problem was, being a Diane Sawyer involves a lot more than sitting in front of a camera. On the fourth day, Nancy Lee didn't show up. She had simply lost interest. She just didn't want it anymore."

"I'll be damned."

Mike caught Rosemary's hasty glance at her watch. He rose to his feet.

"You've been great, Doc," he said. "One more question?"

Rosemary nodded.

"Is Nancy Lee capable of killing? Do you think she would kill to get what she wants?"

Rosemary frowned thoughtfully, then shook her head.

"No," she said. "I don't think Nancy Lee would go so far as to kill in order to get what she wants. Actually, she wouldn't find it necessary. She'd just ask someone to give it to her. And someone would."

"You had me worried for a minute in there." I glanced aside at Mike as I backed out of Doctor Chang's driveway.

"Me? Why?"

"I thought you were going to blow your stack at her. When she snapped at you? Told you not to be ridiculous?"

"Why would I blow my stack? I wasn't angry."

I shifted from reverse into drive and pressed down on the accelerator. "You looked pretty steamed to me."

"What the hell, Cat, I had to do something. When she made that crack about Nancy Lee and AIDS I knew there was more to the story than all that sweetness-and-light hogwash she was feeding us. I didn't know what Nick had on her so I tried throwing a scare into her. If she was afraid of Nick, I figured she wouldn't run the risk of my telling him she'd stiffed me. And it worked, didn't it? Even if it wasn't for the reason I had assumed it would."

"It worked. You were cute as a bug. And if ever I even suspect you of manipulating me like that I'll step on you."

"*Tut, tut,* let's don't be nasty." He chuckled around the cigarette between his lips. "So what do you think?"

"Of what? Rosemary Chang? She seems to be a very nice lady with a rotten sister. Nancy Lee? She's apparently a gorgeous bitch."

"Bitch, I'd agree. But from what you heard, do you think she's a killer?"

"Rosemary doesn't seem to think so. Who knows? Maybe she hired a professional killer."

Mike shook his head. "Professional killers don't stab a body eight times. Speaking of Rosemary, there was something strange about her. Did you notice?"

"No. What?"

"She didn't ask why we were so interested in her sister. Does that seem normal to you? Wouldn't you think she'd be a little bit curious?"

"Maybe she doesn't want to know."

"Or doesn't care."

We rode in silence until I drove into my street.

"I made a pot of stew yesterday," I said. "You want to stay for dinner?"

"Dumplings?" Mike asked hopefully.

"Yeah, yeah. I'll make dumplings."

We were finishing the stew when the phone rang. It was Jenny, calling from the hotel.

"How are you holding up?" I asked.

"I'm okay." Her voice sounded strong. "We're going out for a bite, then I'm hitting the sack. Don't worry. I'm being careful. I don't have much choice. Larry clucks after me like a mother hen."

"Tell him I said to keep it up. How did the day go?"

"Good and bad. The bad—Carmen threw out all my stuff not long after she came back from Spain. She thought I was dead. We're meeting her for lunch tomorrow. Larry's all keen. He saw her do Saint Joan a few years back."

I heard Larry's voice, words indistinguishable, in the background.

"He says Ophelia, not Saint Joan," Jenny reported. "He says she was fantastic. Which she is, incidentally. Anyway, on to the good. I've got my hot little hands on my money and I've applied for new credit cards, no problem. And I have an appointment to meet with Matt Steiner tomorrow morning. He's the agent Hannah was lining me up with."

"You've had a busy day."

"Tomorrow will be busier. We want to get tickets for a show. And don't worry," she added hastily, "I'll sleep in the afternoon."

"When do you plan to get back?"

"Probably the day after tomorrow, Saturday. We've been thinking of staying the weekend, but I don't know. I'll call tomorrow night and let you know. How are things going there?"

"Mike and I, he's here now, met Nancy Lee's sister this afternoon. But it's a long story. I'll tell you about it when you come home. This is costing you money."

"Okay. Say hello to Mike. I'll talk to you tomorrow."

"Goodnight, Jenny. Good luck, tomorrow."

"Thanks, Catherine. Goodnight."

I replaced the phone. It rang immediately.

"Hello, Catherine. It's Nick Kramer." I raised surprised

eyebrows at Mike and mouthed *Nick*. "Is Jenny there? I'd like to speak to her, please."

Mike had half-risen from his chair. I shook my head at him and he sat down again.

"I'm sorry, Nick. She's not here. She's in New York."

"New York?" There was a momentary silence. "Do you know where she's staying?"

"At the Doral. I just spoke to her. She'll probably be back over the weekend. Do you want me to have her call you?"

"It's not necessary, thank you. Did you and Mike get to see Doctor Chang?"

"Yes. Mike's here, Nick. Hang on a second."

I held the phone out to Mike. He took it from me and I went down to the cold room in the basement for a jar of the peaches I had canned last summer. When I returned, he was back at the table, a bemused smile on his face.

He waited until I set a bowl of the peaches in front of him and sat down.

"So Nick's interested in Jenny," he said. "I'd have thought he'd go for a more spectacular type."

"You didn't see Jenny today. She's spectacular."

"Jenny? Spectacular? Come on, Cat. She's no dog, but you have to admit, Kim Basinger she ain't."

"She sure ain't. Jenny's an actress. If the role calls for gorgeous, she turns into gorgeous. And she doesn't just play a tacky little waitress, she *is* a tacky little waitress. Basinger plays Basinger. There's a difference."

"If you say so." Mike had no interest in defending Kim Basinger's talents. His eyes crinkled with gentle amusement. "Do you realize we've got the makings of a good old grade-B movie going here, Cat? Slick Nick, the gangster, meets gentle Jennifer, the artist. Things could get very interesting."

19

Things got very interesting very quickly.

Jenny phoned Friday night to tell me, in a voice combining excitement and apprehension, that they wouldn't return until Sunday. They had run into, of all people, Nick Kramer, purely by accident, when they were leaving the hotel that morning and he had convinced them they should stay the weekend. I was not to worry, she'd get the rest she needed, but it sounded like fun and she wanted to stay. Did I mind?

"Of course I don't mind. Enjoy yourselves." Out of sheer orneriness, I added, "Say hello to Nick for me."

"I will. And I'll call you Sunday morning and let you know which flight we'll be on. Goodnight, Catherine. I've got to run. They're waiting for me."

I replaced the phone, smiling to myself. Slick Nick.

I had spent the entire day in the basement, stripping Charlie's cabinet-on-stand, and I was on my way to bed when Mike phoned. He chortled when I told him about Nick.

"The plot thickens," he said. "I'll bet Nick was outside that hotel at seven in the morning, waiting for her to come out. Larry must have been a surprise. As far as I remember, you didn't mention him when you talked to Nick."

"No, I didn't. Listen, Mike. I'm exhausted. I've got a stripper headache and I'm nauseous from stripper fumes. Unless you're calling with something earth-shattering, can it wait until tomorrow? I'm on my way to bed."

"It'll keep. What do you say we go for a drive in the country tomorrow? The leaves are turning and we can have lunch at that pancake place we found last spring."

"I'd like that."

"I'll pick you up at nine o'clock."

I took a couple of aspirins and set the alarm. I didn't want to wake up late. Mike is obsessively punctual. Actually, he is obsessively early, a hangover from his newspaper days, I suppose, but he doesn't begin to get testy until one minute after the time designated.

He was ten minutes early, and in a cheerful mood. There was no argument as to who would drive. He parked his car, got into the passenger seat in mine, and immediately lit a cigarette. He puffed serenely and said nothing until we were out of city traffic and cruising the freeway.

"Okay." He butted his cigarette, adjusted his seat belt so he could face me more comfortably. "Ready?"

"Let 'er rip."

"First of all, in spite of what Rosemary Chang said, I was convinced Nancy Lee killed Jason Cody. She never divorced him, she married rich, and he tried to blackmail her."

"But you don't know she never . . ."

"Cat, don't interrupt. We can go into the ifs, ands, or buts later. I want to give you the sequence and I don't want to leave anything out. Bear with me, all right?"

"I'll be quiet as a mouse back here, sir."

"So I went to the *Gazette* to check out the file for November eighth, the night Jason was killed, just on the off-chance there might be some reference to Nancy Lee donating her charitable presence to some winging that night. And sure enough there was. Nancy Lee was on the guest list the *Gazette* printed of a DAR dinner, held in honor of the outgoing president. Which blew my theory right out of the water."

Mike paused for dramatic effect. I opened my mouth to speak, thought better of it, and concentrated on my driving.

"I checked out November ninth, the night somebody tried for Jenny, but Nancy Lee must have stayed home that night. So I went back to the previous weekend paper and went through it, page by page, and who do I find on page twenty-two but Morley Richards. There he is, cutting the ribbon for a Gay Community Center to which he contributed half a million bucks."

I had to ask, "Who is Morley Richards?"

"He's one of the old men in Jason's *feelthy peechers*, remember? The one Charlie gave the pictures to? As far as I'm concerned, old Morley is still a contender. Anyway, I had the entire paper statted. When does Jenny get back?"

"Sunday."

"I want her to go through it. There could be something she would recognize that I wouldn't know about."

"I'm not sure what time she'll be back. She said she'd call me Sunday morning. I'll let you know."

Mike nodded. "Okay. Now, on to the juicy part. On my way out of the building I ran into Kitty Drummond. Kitty's the society page editor."

I shot a wide-eyed glance sideways. "She's still around? Migod, she must be a thousand years old. We used her in a commercial I produced at least twenty years ago and she was no spring chicken then. I remember her as an insufferable snob with a massive *grande-dame* complex."

Mike chuckled. "That's her act and it's a damn good one. Actually, she's a good type and one hell of a competent newspaperman. Pardon me, newspaperwoman. We did a fair amount of pub-crawling together back in the days when I was writing my column. She's over seventy now and she knows where all the upper-crust bodies are buried, going back ten generations."

Mike lit a cigarette, inhaled deeply, and sent out a stream of fragrant blue smoke.

"On impulse," he continued, "I asked her if it was possible there could have been a mistake made in a DAR guest list a year ago. You'd have thought I'd rammed a poker up her butt. She's a pro, and she's damn proud of that page of hers. We went up to her office. She dug into her computer and brought up the list and asked me what the hell kind of mistake was I talking about. I said I had reason to believe Nancy Lee Manville had not attended the dinner. She read the list over a couple of times. She closed her eyes. Then she told me Nancy Lee had been there, that she'd worn a black silk chiffon dress with a big white lace collar."

"She remembered that? I don't believe it."

"I know. I said the same thing. She told me, if she thought about it long enough, she could describe what Caroline Manville wore to her engagement party, forty years ago. Then, and I'm quoting her—Kitty's got a mouth like a sewer—she said, 'Okay, Mike, you devious son of a bitch, what the fuck is this all about?' So I told her."

"You told her?" I took my eyes off the road and glared at Mike. "About Jenny? What if she tells . . ."

"Hey!" Mike barked, "Give me credit for a couple of smarts, Cat. I know Kitty. She's got more secrets locked away than the CIA. Besides, it paid off."

"How?"

"I'll get to it. To begin with, what Rosemary told us was her version of the truth. Her father didn't just die, he committed suicide after he'd pissed away the Rountree fortune playing big-time entrepreneur. Kitty says he was the local mark for every hustler who came down the pike with a fast line and a salted gold mine."

"Poor Rosemary. I guess she has to believe whatever she can live with."

"Don't we all. Anyway, Kitty says his birdbrained wife wasn't left penniless, as Rosemary led us to believe. She still has Quincy money. It's been watered down some since old Doc Quincy traded his ninety-percent-alcohol Magic Elixir to the Indians for furs, but a welfare candidate she's not."

"Rosemary said there was no money for college."

"Money's relative. I suppose when you're down to your last million you might start pinching pennies."

"I suppose. What about the Manvilles?"

"It seems the first Manville was a horse trader who made his pile during the Civil War. They're still horsey people. That's how Ham Junior and Nancy Lee met, at the Hunt Club. Ham took one look at Nancy Lee with her legs spread over a horse and blew like a stud stallion. He couldn't get into her britches without the proper papers, so he married her. According to Kitty, Nancy Lee spends like the keys to Fort

Knox came with the name and Ham's as tight as a virgin's twat—pardon me, Cat, I'm quoting Kitty. So now Ham'd like to unload her and he can't."

"Why not?"

"Because she'd take half the Manville money with her."

"Can she do that? I thought rich people signed papers or something when they got married."

"Kitty says she can. And since the only thing the Manvilles love more than their horses is their money, everybody makes nice and the money stays where it belongs."

Mike rolled the window down to flick his cigarette out, realized we were driving through a country lane, and butted it in the ashtray.

"And that's the payoff, Cat."

"What is?"

"The fact that the Manvilles, given any legal out, would dump Nancy Lee like a load of steaming horseshit. If Nancy Lee did forget to divorce Jason, the marriage to Ham isn't valid. She wouldn't get a dime. And Ham could lay charges. Bigamy is a no-no."

I shook my head. "I just can't see her forgetting. You heard what Rosemary said. Nancy Lee is no dummy."

"I heard what Rosemary said. Nancy Lee has a high IQ. She's also a head case who believes her actions are exempt from the natural law of consequence. Forgetting might be the wrong word. Not bothering is probably more like it."

"Mike, you keep belaboring the assumption that there was no divorce." The pancake house appeared as we rounded a curve and I slowed down. "You don't know that. You just like it because it fits your scenario."

"Damn right I like it." Mike loosened his seat belt as I pulled into the parking lot. "And I've got ten bucks that says I'm right."

"No bet."

"Piker."

Throughout lunch we discussed the ifs, the ands, and the buts, including those pertaining to Morley Richards. When we emerged from the restaurant, peacefully sated, the clouds marring the drive up had vanished, leaving the sky a limpid aqua. A mellow autumn sun beamed its slanted rays, casting deep purple shadows on the golden hills.

We rode home in companionable silence, speaking only to point out the vermilion flare of a maple, the dramatic effect of a yellowing birch floating against a background of green-black pines.

In the rearview mirror I caught a glimpse of a V-string of Canada geese and pulled over to the sandy shoulder of the road. We climbed out of the car to listen as they passed high overhead. Heads tilted to the sky, we watched until they were specks in the distance, no longer heard.

"That's the most beautiful and the most exciting and the most yearning sound I know," Mike said softly after they had disappeared. "There's something about the way they call that sets me trembling inside."

I nodded. "I know. Their call and the cry of the loon. Haunting. And wild."

"Gypsy music."

We were about to return to our seats in the car when a black cloud of crows exploded from the stubble field beside us. Wheeling and circling in unison above us, their raucous squawking shredded the tranquil autumn air.

Mike grinned at me across the hood of the car.

"Heavy metal," he said.

20

The persistent ringing of a telephone, merging with the measured *bong bong* of a church bell, dragged me from a dream of endless prairie lying breathless under a blue dome of sky. I was barefoot, a child again, squatting in a dusty lane, intent on a stream of black ants frantically maneuvering the husk of a dead grasshopper.

I awoke, disoriented. The phone rang twice more before I was able to recall my wandering soul back into my body. I slid from bed and plodded to the kitchen.

"Catherine!" Jenny's husky voice sang in my ear. "I was just about to hang up!"

"What time is it?" I peered blearily at the clock. "What *day* is it?"

"I woke you. I'm sorry," Jenny apologized. "I just wanted to tell you we have an afternoon flight. We should arrive there at five. You don't have to meet us. Nick's car is at the airport. He'll bring us home."

"Fine." I gathered my thoughts. "Jenny? Mike will be here, he wants to talk to you. Ask Nick if he'd like to join us for dinner."

"Hold it."

I listened to muffled conversation, my eye on the clock. Nine-thirty? I had slept a full twelve hours? The bells from the seminary down the street provided the day. Sunday.

"Catherine? Nick says he'd like to very much. But you're not to cook. He'll have dinner sent from the Capri. That's a restaurant he owns."

"I know. Tell Nick he's a gentleman and a scholar and I accept with gratitude."

Four seconds ticked by, then Jenny, somewhat dubiously, said, "I'll tell him exactly that. See you later."

At precisely five o'clock, while I was digging paste varnish from under my fingernails, a white van, with *Capri* scripted in blue on the side panels, arrived in my driveway. I dried my hands and went to the front door.

A short, muscular-looking young man with black hair, dark eyes, a dusky Mediterranean complexion, and the whitest of smiles, carried four cobalt-blue boxes and a straw-covered bottle of Chianti into my kitchen.

"Put the manicotti in the oven at two-fifty, keep it warm, Vittorio told me to tell you. The antipasto and the insalata in the fridge, the gelato in the freezer. The wine, she's fine. Okay?"

He refused the tip I offered, telling me it had been taken care of, gave me a broad, sweet smile, a cheerful ciao, and was gone.

I had time to change into clean jeans and shirt and set the table before everyone arrived, almost simultaneously. Mike, walking into the kitchen, gestured toward the front of the house.

"Nick's parking on the street," he said. "No room in the driveway. They'll be right in."

Jenny looked smashing, no other word would do.

Her makeup was flawless. Green jade teardrops hung from her earlobes. Her belted trench coat, the same red-gold as her hair, was of buttery suede, with deep raglan sleeves. Her sweater was cashmere, in a shade of green matched exactly to the exquisite earrings. Narrow, loden-green pants were tucked into matching leather boots.

Mike stared, then whistled softly.

Jenny looked momentarily startled, then smiled and gave a small mock curtsy. She untied the belt of her coat. "I hope dinner arrived. Nick wouldn't let us eat plane food. We're starving."

"It arrived," I said. "Thank you, Nick. It was very considerate of you."

"My pleasure." Nick nodded. He helped Jenny slip out of her coat, then handed the coat to Larry, who disappeared, I assumed, to hang it in Jenny's bedroom closet.

The interaction intrigued me. Had a pecking order been established in New York?

I set out the antipasto, gave Nick a corkscrew and the bottle of wine, and we sat down together. Throughout dinner, while Jenny and Larry chattered about shows and shopping, I observed more than I listened.

The tension between Nick and Jenny was almost palpable. He watched her from under those extravagant lashes with the focus that had so unnerved me when I first met him a year ago. Jenny, more animated than I had ever seen her, glanced at him often but skittered away from prolonged eye contact.

At one point, agreeing with Larry on some difference of opinion, Nick placed his hand on Jenny's shoulder, an oddly proprietary gesture. For no reason, I looked at Mike. He raised his eyebrows at me.

Larry, beaming on them, was obviously approving of the smouldering current flowing between his two beautiful people. His smiles evoked images of a benign duenna whose charges were behaving well. He and Nick seemed to have established an easy, bantering relationship whose aim was to amuse Jenny.

It also cut the turgid air to a breathable level.

When I rose to clear the table and make coffee, Mike brought out the *Gazette* stats. He handed them to Jenny and asked her to go through them carefully, page by page. He recounted our meeting with Doctor Chang, the information he had gleaned from Kitty Drummond.

"You still believe Nancy Lee killed Jason Cody?" Nick asked when Mike finished.

Mike nodded. "I don't know why, Nick, but I've got a gut feeling about this woman. I'd like to get a look at her. Find out where she hangs out and just get a look at her."

"We can do better than that," Nick said.

"Yeah? How?"

"The Hunt Club Costume Ball for Cancer Research is this coming Friday. I have a table reserved. I don't always attend, but I always buy a table. Nancy Lee will be there. We can go, if you like."

Mike was genuinely surprised. "Why would you buy a table at a Hunt Club shindig?"

"I suppose because I'm a member, Pop." Nick's eyes were amused. "Do you want to go or not?"

"If Nancy Lee will be there, I want to go. Why don't we all go? Will your table accommodate the five of us?"

"Easily." Nick smiled suddenly and I realized how rarely I have seen him smile. "You'll have to wear a costume, Mike."

"Big deal." Mike shrugged. "I'll go as a clown."

21

Rena called early next morning.

"I have the handles for your cabinet," she said. "They're not exactly the same as the ones you have but they're in the same family. I think they'll do."

"Can I pick them up?"

"That's why I'm calling. I have a doctor's appointment at eleven. If you can come now?"

"I'll be there in half an hour."

Rena was right, the handles were a perfect replacement. I thanked her and we had our customary argument over what I should pay, she insisting she only wanted her money back, I determined to pay the price she would have charged at the flea market.

She gave in too easily. I thought she looked tired and asked about the appointment with her doctor.

"Just a virus." She dismissed my concern. "I'm overdue for a checkup anyway."

We parted company at her door, waving to each other as we passed in our separate cars.

I stopped at a market to restock green vegetables, milk, and liver for Jenny. When I reached home, I found Larry's Mercedes parked in the driveway. He was in the kitchen, scrambling eggs, listening unabashedly to Jenny's phone conversation.

"Sounds fabulous!" She waved at me, her eyes bright with excitement. "Great. I'll see you tonight."

She hung up. "That was Matt." She exulted. I must have looked blank. "Matt Steiner! My new agent," she explained. "He's got one of the soap mags hot on doing a cover story about me. Amanda Prentiss lives! Jennifer Steele's mystery year! Some crap like that. A *cover* story, Catherine! Larry, do you believe it?"

"Fantastic!" Larry abandoned the stove and threw his arms around Jenny. "Let the games begin!"

"Congratulations, Jen." I set the bag of groceries on the table and hurried to rescue the eggs from scorching. "Did I hear you say you'd see him tonight?"

"He has me booked on the four-thirty flight. He wants to prep me tonight. Our meeting with the soap people is first thing in the morning." The phone rang. Without thinking, she snatched it up and caroled, "Hallo-oh?"

Her face changed. Her body shifted slightly and Larry let his arms drop.

"Hello, Nick," she said huskily. She listened a moment, her head lowered. "I'm sorry, I can't. Matt just called. I'm taking the four-thirty flight. I'll be in New York tonight."

She turned away from us, the phone pressed to her ear. "I'm not sure. Tomorrow, maybe. Maybe Wednesday. I don't know what Matt has . . ." She paused, then said. "Yes. Yes, I will. Good-bye, Nick."

She replaced the phone thoughtfully, her hand lingering. She turned to face us, her gaze directed at Larry.

"Come with me," she said.

Larry shook his head. "Jenny, two's company. Three's a crowd. Nick's going, isn't he?"

"I don't think so. He didn't say anything about going. He just asked me to let him know when I'll be back."

"He'll be there."

"Come anyway."

"Not this time."

"Why? Don't you like Nick?"

"I adore Nick." Larry grinned at her, a deliberately lascivious leer. "If you don't want him, I'll take him off your hands anytime."

Jenny laughed. "What a mensch."

"Anything for a friend." Larry shrugged. "Besides, I couldn't go if I wanted to. Somebody's got to find costumes for us for Friday."

I prepared lunch while the two of them packed for Jenny. I could hear them arguing over what she should wear for the interview in the morning. Except for Larry's deeper male voice, they sounded like girlfriends planning for the prom.

"What do you think, Cat?" Larry pushed Jenny ahead of him into the kitchen.

She was dressed in the blond trench coat, worn over a black cowl-neck sweater dress. Black hose, black shoes, black satchel handbag. Black sunglasses. Her hair was parted in the center, allowed to fall naturally, framing her face.

"Very dramatic." I hedged.

"Very sharp," Larry said. "She looks like a star."

"Larry. I look like a goddamn spy," Jenny snarled cheerfully. "What do you think, Catherine? Does this getup look sharp to you?"

"You're asking me? I haven't known what sharp looks like since nineteen seventy-five." I set the salad bowl on the table. "Lunch, kiddies."

Lunch was good-natured quibbling about what sort of costumes Larry was to look for. Then Jenny went to lie down for an hour, Larry went shopping for the pantyhose and hairspray she needed, and I went to the basement to rub a second coat of varnish on Charlie's cabinet.

When he returned, Larry came down to the basement.

"Jen's getting dressed," he said. "Are you coming to the airport with us?"

"I hadn't planned to. Why? Do you think I should?"

"Not unless you're crazy for airports." He ran his palm over the cabinet's satiny surface. "This is beautiful," he said. "When do you want to deliver it?"

"I'm hoping tomorrow."

"You'll need a hand getting it up the stairs. I'll come over in the morning, if you like."

"Thank you, Larry." I was touched by his thoughtfulness. "I'd really appreciate it."

"No problem. I'll work it into my crowded schedule."

* * *

Larry was as good as his word. Next morning, we loaded the cabinet into my station wagon and he followed me to Canterbury House.

Charlie greeted him with a benign smile.

"Ah. The prodigal returns! Hey, Rafe, where the hell do we find a sacrificial lamb?"

"You've got the menu wrong, Charlie," Larry corrected cheerfully. "Prodigals get fatted calf."

"Well, bless your cotton socks. How would a nice Jewish boy like you know something like that?" He patted Larry's cheek with obvious affection. "Good to see you, kiddo. We've missed your pretty face around here, haven't we, Rafe?"

"The coffee's been gut-wrenching." As always, Rafe's frozen one-sided smile was deceptively cynical. "Even the customers are complaining."

Larry laughed. "Charlie's always too heavy-handed with the chicory. I'll make some, if you like."

"Like? I'd love." As Larry went to the offices at the rear of the store, Rafe added, "It surprises me, but I really miss the kid, you know?"

"I know," I agreed. "He sort of grows on you."

"What a ghastly thought." Charlie shuddered. "Apropos of malignant growths, what about Orphan Annie? What's the porno pictures story? Where on earth did she get them?"

I brought them up to date. Charlie's mouth turned down with distaste when I mentioned the Manvilles.

"Caroline Manville's a customer of ours. Typical old-money horsey set. Always trying to get it for nothing."

"What about Nancy Lee? Do you know her?"

Charlie shook his head. "Not really. She wafts in and out with Caroline on occasion, but, as she so sweetly puts it, antiques aren't really her thing. I have the impression Nancy Lee's only thing is Nancy Lee. Gorgeous, of course, but a total space puppy."

"Mike claims he has this gut feeling about her. We're going to a costume ball Friday so he can get a look at her."

"The Hunt Club costume ball?" Charlie asked, surprised. "We'll see you there, then."

"You're going?"

"Contacts, Cat. Strictly business. For a thousand bucks a head we get to rub bums with a bunch of horse's asses."

"Which is about as much fun as an enema," Rafe added. "Speaking of business, Cat. We have a nice Regency hall chair that needs some work. No stripping, the mahogany's fine, but the seat tapestry is threadbare. You interested?"

"Let's take a look at it."

We went to the workroom at the rear of the store. The chair was beautiful, with a high carved back and graceful cabriole legs. It deserved the best. I ran through my fabric inventory in my mind.

"I think I have something that'll work," I said. "A wool needlepoint. The background is Wedgwood blue. The center is cabbage roses done in *petit-point*."

"Sounds good." Rafe nodded.

"It'll cost you, Rafe."

"No problem. Do you think we can have it Friday?'

"If I take it now, sure."

Larry poked his head through the open doorway. "Coffee's ready, Rafe. In your office."

"Thanks, Larry. Stay for coffee, Cat?"

"I think I'll get along home, Rafe. Thanks, anyway."

"Larry?"

"Not me. I'm going costume shopping."

Jenny phoned just after eleven.

"I didn't wake you, did I?" she asked apologetically. "We just got back to the hotel."

We? "No, it's okay. I was watching the news. How did it go today?"

"Lots of yakking. A photo session. I spent most of the day in front of a camera. Matt wants new stills." She sounded gratified, but weary.

"Sounds good. When do you expect to be home?"

"That's why I'm calling. Matt got a commercial for me,

we'll be shooting tomorrow. And I'm scheduled for a talk show on Thursday, the day the soap mag hits the stands. I won't be back until Friday. I'm booked on the seven A.M. flight."

"Would you like me to call Larry and let him know when you're coming? Or Nick?"

"Thanks, Catherine. I'll call Larry." For two seconds there was silence on the line, then she added the words I was already anticipating: "Nick's here."

22

I'm convinced there are days when God gets thoroughly pissed off with the way we're running his world and pumps bile into the ozone.

Friday had to be one of those days.

A chilling rain drizzled down from the leaden skies. Loading Rafe's chair into the station wagon in old, worn-smooth sneakers, I slipped on the wet grass and cracked my skull on the open tailgate door. I gritted my teeth and shoved the chair to safety inside the wagon, then slammed the offending door viciously.

Clutching my throbbing head, I was headed back to the house when Larry's stupid little car spun down the driveway. The rear wheel sent up a spray of puddle water, drenching me to the knees.

He climbed out of the car, his mood no better than mine.

"Idiots," he said angrily. "They've lost her suitcase. We've been hanging around the damn airport for two hours. God knows where it went, those airline jerks sure don't."

Jenny emerged from the passenger side of the car. She looked pale and tired.

"Forget it, Larry," she said. "It isn't worth getting into a sweat about. I can get along without it. It'll show up sooner or later."

They followed me into the house, into the kitchen, Jenny trudging wearily, Larry stomping. I felt like Mother Goose.

"Have you had breakfast?"

"No." Larry's anger had cooled. He smiled. "I was too damn mad to eat."

"I'm not hungry," Jenny said.

"Hungry or not, you're going to eat something. Larry,

there's fresh fruit salad in the fridge. Make some toast and a pot of tea and see that Jen eats before she lies down. I'm leaving to deliver Rafe's chair. I should be back by noon."

I arrived at Canterbury House to find Charlie and Rafe snarling at each other. I unloaded the chair and beat a retreat before I could be drawn into their argument.

The drive home, which should have been peaceful, turned out to be a war of the roads.

A truck had wedged itself in the first underpass and I was trapped in the long line of cars waiting to gain access to the thruway. I sat for half an hour, breathing exhaust fumes and watching the truck driver jump periodically from his cab to give the finger to the senselessly bleating horns. Help arrived in time to save him from being pounded into the pavement by an avenging group of irate drivers.

Once on the thruway, I relaxed. Until a black van, changing lanes on a sudden and irrational impulse, missed sideswiping me by inches. Mildly shaken, I moved into the slow lane and found myself hemmed in by behemoths; a moving van two-stories high ahead, a trailerload of shiny cars on my left, the toothy radiator of some giant in my rearview mirror, all moving at a relentless speed.

When the van made an exit, I tramped the accelerator to fill the void in front, almost colliding with a small blue car that decided to change lanes without signalling.

Safely past, I had the eerie notion that no human beings were piloting the traffic. The cars themselves, infected by some destructive virus, were on a rampage. Playing with the thought got me home, reasonably sane.

There was a note from Larry on the kitchen table.

I've gone to the airport. They found the bag. Jen's asleep. Mike called. He wants you to call him. Thought I'd pick up Chinese on the way back and we'd have dinner together before we get dressed up. Is that okay with you?

Larry

Okay with me? If he'd been near, I'd have hugged him. I picked up the phone and dialed Mike.

"Where've you been?" he demanded when I said hello.

"Oh, hell. *Et tu, Brute!*" I said.

"What? What d'you mean?"

"I mean the world seems to be in a very strange and filthy mood today."

"The hell with the mood of the world. My starting motor just died and the garage won't take me till Monday."

"You want me to pick you up?"

"What I want to know is the where, when, and how tonight. Is Nick meeting us, or what?"

"I don't know what Nick planned." I thought a moment. "Look, Larry's bringing Chinese food for dinner. Why don't I ask him to pick you up? We can eat here and all go together."

"Hell, he doesn't have to pick me up. I'll take a cab." Mike paused. "If you don't mind, I'll bring my costume and change at your place. Getting into a cab in a clown outfit isn't my idea of cute. What are you wearing?"

The question stopped me cold. For some peculiar reason, until that moment, it had not occurred to me I would have to wear a costume, too.

"I don't know. I haven't thought . . ." An idea popped into my head, an easy out. "Mike? Have you got a big, ratty, faded old cardigan I can borrow?"

"I could probably dig one up. Why?"

"I'm going as a bag lady."

Mike hooted in my ear. "You wouldn't," he said.

"Why not? You've got to admit I know what the real thing looks like. And I've got the worn-out sneakers. I've got the threadbare jeans, plus at least a dozen paint-stained, ragged sweatshirts. If you can find a ratty old sweater for me, all I'll need is a tacky toque and some dirt."

"You don't think Jenny will be offended?"

"Why would she . . ." I stopped and thought. "That'll be interesting. Her reaction. Do you think she'll be upset?"

"I don't really see any reason why she should be. But I

don't know, Cat. I don't know her well enough."

"Maybe I'll check with Larry first. Although I don't know what I'll wear if he doesn't think it's a good idea."

"You can always go as a stripper. Yuk yuk."

"Good-bye, Mike."

Larry arrived with Jenny's suitcase and an armload of white cartons.

I told him about the bag lady getup. "What do you think, Larry? You know her better than anybody."

"I do?" His eyes lit up. "Really?"

"Who else? So, what do you think? Yes or no?"

"I think she'll get a blast out of it."

"I hope you're right."

Mike brought me a dirty old cardigan and a faded red wool-knit hat with a crumpled visor and earflaps.

"I don't care about the sweater," he said. "But don't lose the hat. I'm very sentimental about that hat. It's the first thing Nick ever asked me to buy for him."

"Do you think he'll recognize it?"

"I doubt it."

The phone rang. I picked it up, listened, then laughed. It was Nick.

"What's funny?" he asked.

"Mike and I were just talking about you. Where are you?"

"Still in New York. I missed my earlier flight. I'll meet you in the hotel lobby tonight, all right? I'll wait for you if I get there first. Tell Jenny, would you?"

"Sure, Nick. And we'll wait in the lobby if we get there before you do."

"Good. They're calling my flight. See you later."

Jenny woke refreshed. As we ate dinner, she told us about the cast of characters in the green room, where guests on the talk show waited to appear. They all sounded very, very strange.

At seven-thirty I pushed away from the table.

"You three go get changed. I'm going to clean up this mess. Then I want the bathroom to myself for ten minutes."

Mike didn't even leave the kitchen. He pulled a white tent suit, spattered with large varicolored dots, over his clothing, fastened a white ruff around his neck, and fitted a bright orange fright wig over his balding head.

"Ta da!" He handed me a lipstick. "Now, m'dear, if you'd kindly paint a couple of big red spots on me cheeks, I'll be ready to go to the ball."

He sat in a chair and tilted his head back. Instead of spots, I lipsticked a big red heart on each cheek.

"I forgot to tell you," I said, "Charlie and Rafe will be there." I painted a red dot on his nose, another on his chin. "There, you're done. You look lovely."

"I feel like a horse's ass."

"Then you'll be right at home. According to Charlie, you'll be spending the evening with a bunch of them."

He looked past me and said, "Wow!"

Jenny and Larry pranced down the hall, side by side, matching their steps and their arm movements.

Their harlequin costumes were identical. Bronze ballet slippers, shiny tights in a bronze, pearlescent white, gold, and silver diamond pattern. Billowing blousons of the same fabric. Frothy gold lace ruffs framed their powdered faces, gold skull caps hid their hair. And on their right cheeks glittered a huge rhinestone teardrop.

They struck a pose in the kitchen doorway. Mike and I applauded.

"Sensational!" I said.

"You'll knock 'em dead," Mike promised. "Okay, Cat, get a move on. Let's get this show on the road."

It took me all of five minutes to change my clothes, smear Vaseline into my hair, and rub dirt from a hibiscus plant over my face. I stuffed towels into a jute bag, topped them with a dirty T-shirt, pulled Nick's toque on my greasy head, and shuffled into the kitchen.

Jenny's eyes widened. Then she burst into laughter.

"My God," she said. "Is that how I looked?"

"It's close." I smiled. "You're not mad?"

"Why would I be mad?" She grinned back at me. "But you forgot something."

"What?"

"The smell's missing. You don't stink."

23

The parking area of the Four Seasons, a new hotel not far from the airport, was crowded. We managed to find a space, wide enough to accommodate Larry's car and my wagon, toward the rear of the lot.

The rain had ended earlier, the clouds had dispersed, and we walked to the hotel entrance under a deep indigo sky, heavy with stars. The night air smelled sweetly of early autumn, cool and clean.

There was no sign of Nick in the lobby. We sat down to wait and watched Charlie and Rafe make an entrance, Charlie as a swashbuckling, one-eyed pirate and Rafe as the semi-masked Phantom of the Opera.

"My, my," Charlie said as he greeted us, "aren't we the creative ones. A clown and a frump. And you two." He turned his yellow eye on Larry and Jenny. "You look like a set of salt-and-pepper shakers."

"Come on, Charlie," Rafe said wearily. "Knock it off."

Charlie bristled. For a moment he glared at Rafe, at us, then he relaxed visibly.

"Aw, shit. I'm sorry, you guys," he apologized. "It's just been one bitch of a day. I'm sorry."

"Forget it, Charlie." Mike waved Charlie's bad temper into the past. "We all know you're an obnoxious prick. We love you anyway."

Charlie smiled whitely through his black beard. "Ah, Mike," he said, "you silver-tongued clown, you. What say we gang up? We can sit together and amuse ourselves taking pot-shots at the rich kids."

"I like it." Mike laughed. "We're waiting for Nick to get

here. He has a reserved table. If there's room, we can all sit together."

"A reserved table? *Ooh-la-la.*" Charlie's eyebrow lifted. "I'm impressed. Who the hell is Nick?"

"Nick Kramer. You met him last year, remember? When Cat was playing hardball with the Mafia?"

"We didn't meet him, Mike," Rafe interjected. "You told us about him. But we've never met him."

"You're going to meet him now. The riverboat gambler who just came through the revolving door? That's Nick."

Nick, looking spectacularly handsome in a planter's hat, flowing black bow tie, deep sideburns, and a trim Clark Gable mustache, came striding toward us, his gaze shifting quizzically between Jenny and Larry.

"A matched pair." He smiled on reaching us. He placed his hand unerringly on Jenny's shoulder. "You look fabulous. You, too, Larry. Hello, Catherine, Mike. Sorry I'm late."

"You're not late," Mike said. "Nick, I'd like you to meet a couple of good friends. The pirate is Charlie Harwood, the Phantom is Rafe Verdoni. I've asked them to join us, if there's room at your table."

"Plenty of room. The table's for eight." Nick, shaking Charlie's hand, then Rafe's, surprised me by adding, "You're Canterbury House Antiques, aren't you?"

"You know our shop?" Charlie asked, equally startled.

"The best pieces in my jade collection came from you. Your celadon Qing Dynasty dragon was my first."

Rafe frowned. "The Qing dragon? I seem to remember selling the dragon at the Wintergarden Show. To an elderly Asian gentleman."

Nick nodded. "A friend." He turned, smiling, to the rest of us. "Shall we go up?" he said.

The ballroom was on the mezzanine floor. We stepped off the escalator into a noisy, costumed crowd ebbing and flowing around the wide entrance to the ballroom beyond. Strung out like ducklings, we followed Nick through jostling bodies to the doorway where a portly, red-faced man, dressed in a silk top hat, black riding jacket, and pale jodhpurs, officiously demanded credentials.

"Kramer," Nick said curtly. "Table four."

"Ah, yes, Mr. Kramer." The man's cheeks bunched, his lips spread in a beaming, Toby-Jug smile. "We're absolutely delighted you could come."

He snapped his fingers at a group of giggling teenage girls wearing pink hunting jackets and black-velvet riding helmets. One of the girls detached herself and hurried over to us.

"This is Melissa Hardinge. She will escort you to your table."

Melissa flashed a steel-retainer grin and led us to a round table situated next to the large dance floor. As we seated ourselves the ten-piece orchestra facing us began to play, of all things, "Elmer's Tune." Mike and I looked at each other and laughed. There'd be no lambada tonight.

The dance floor filled quickly. The band segued to "Mrs. Robinson," and the dancers, none of whom appeared to be under forty, flowed past us—devils, clowns, Cleopatras, a chubby Marie Antoinette whose towering wig kept slipping, pilgrims, the Washingtons, three Abe Lincolns of varying height and leanness, a very *zaftig* Mae West, a dozen pirates, a dozen gypsies, a dozen belly dancers who should have known better.

After "Lemon Tree" and "Aquarius" and three solid thumps on the bass drum, the tempo changed. The band slipped into the silky strains of "Spanish Eyes." With the slower music, the dance floor became less frenetic.

"Want to try it now?" Nick smiled at Jenny.

She nodded. They rose together. Nick took her in his arms and danced her adroitly into the passing stream.

After they had vanished, Charlie rapped the table with his knuckles.

"You know how much this table cost him?" he demanded of Mike. "Your friend Nick? Ten thousand bucks!"

"*Ten thousand!*" Mike's clown face was incredulous. "Jesus Christ, no wonder that cretin at the door kissed his ass. You sure?"

"The four tables across here." Charlie indicated the other three tables situated along the dance floor. "The Hardinge's, the Papadacos's, the Manville's. The Manvilles don't seem to be here yet. But these four tables? Ten big ones each."

Mike shrugged. "He can afford it."

"He can? What the hell does he . . ." Charlie began, then interrupted himself. "Hey. There's Morley Richards. He's heading this way. Isn't that one of the dirty old men with him?"

It was the hairy one. He was taller than he had appeared in the photos, both he and Morley were over six feet tall. He was heavier than he had seemed but he looked younger than I remembered. Morley could have passed for fifty. This man didn't seem much older. Both wore brown monastic cassocks draped with oversized wooden rosaries.

The two of them bore down on Charlie. Charlie smiled up at them. "Hello, Morley," he said. "Great costume."

Morley didn't return the smile. "We want the negatives, Charlie," he said, his tone insultingly abrupt.

"*We* do?" Charlie was suddenly Charles, haughtily cool. "And who, may I ask, is we?"

The hairy one's face darkened. "I'm René Junot. And we want those negatives. Now."

"René Junot. Ah, yes. New Orleans. Well, René Junot from New Orleans, you're just going to have to ask my friend Mike here about that." He tilted his head at Mike. "Michael, my dear, these people want the negatives of those reprehensible snapshots you gave me. Make them ask nicely."

Mike had been watching Charlie with amusement. He shook his head at the two men. "There are no negatives," he said.

Junot's arm flashed. He grabbed the ruff around Mike's neck in a hairy paw and twisted. Rafe and Charlie were on their feet before he could speak.

"Morley." Rafe's voice was low. "Tell your friend to back off. He's making a spectacle of himself. This could all get very ugly, very fast. I promise you, we'll check it out and call you in the morning."

Morley hesitated, then nodded. "Okay, Rafe. Come on, René. Rafe's right. Let's go."

Junot released Mike with obvious reluctance. He glared at Charlie and turned to walk away with Morley.

"Hey, René!" Mike called after his receding back, "by any chance were you in town last November? Early November?"

Junot stopped dead. Morley, a step behind, placed his hand in the middle of Junot's back and pushed him on.

Charlie chuckled. "Mr. Junot from New Orleans seems to have a very short fuse."

"You were baiting him, you moron." Rafe dropped back into his chair. "Goddammit, Charlie, why do you always have to be such a shit disturber?"

"Because it's fun, you twit. Dispels the old ennui. Look at poor old Larry. Bored out of his skull." Charlie grabbed Larry's hand and pulled him to his feet. "C'mon you purdy l'il thang, you. Let's get away from these old fuds."

He whisked a startled Larry onto the dance floor. They were swallowed up immediately.

"What's with Charlie?" I asked Rafe. "If I didn't know better I'd swear he was high."

"His birthday's coming up."

"So his birthday's coming up. Don't tell me Charlie's one of those people who thinks getting old isn't going to happen to them."

"Hell, no." Rafe smiled. "Charlie's looking forward to being a crotchety old man. He's already got his crusty old codger act worked out."

"So? What's wrong with his birthday?"

"His family. *You're breaking Mother's heart, Charles.* We go through this every year."

"For Christ's sake." Mike leaned into the conversation. "You two have been together longer than most marriages last. Charlie has to be pushing sixty. They still haven't accepted that he is what he is?"

"They never will, Mike. They're clinging to a world they know." Rafe shrugged. "Don't we all."

The band's signature *thump-thump-thump* marked the end of

the set. Several couples drifted from the floor, Nick and Jenny among them. Rafe and Mike rose from their chairs as Jenny approached the table. Rafe, facing the entrance to the ballroom, nudged Mike.

"You wanted to get a look at Nancy Lee? Look over toward the door. The Manville menagerie has arrived."

I craned my neck to see without standing but there was too much activity blocking my view. It wasn't until they were approaching along the perimeter of the dance floor that I had a good look at them.

They were a group of eight, led by a handsome, fiftyish woman, dressed in medieval costume, her hair hidden under a blue chiffon wimple and a narrow gold crown.

"The Queen Guenivere character is Caroline Manville." Rafe spoke in an undertone. "The big woman in the Roman toga getup is Adele Rountree, Nancy Lee's mother. The French dandy is Hamilton Manville. The four in Robin Hood outfits are the Prescotts. She was a Manville, old Ham's sister."

Caroline Manville stopped to chat two tables down and the group shifted, the Prescotts breaking rank and moving toward their table next to ours.

"Ah," Rafe said. "There she is. That's Nancy Lee."

For a split second I was disappointed. She was small, five-three at most, and she didn't exude presence as did Caroline Manville. Then, as she drew nearer, following in the wake of her mother-in-law, I felt the full impact of her perfection.

She was dressed as Madame Récamier in an exquisitely simple white chiffon Empire gown. Her white-blond hair was piled and bound with pearls, with tendrils artfully released to frame the almost perfect oval of her face.

Her eyes, almond-shaped and large, were an incredible shade of deep turquoise. Her lips were palest pink. Her skin was as creamy and glowing as the pearls twined in her hair. Seeing her, I recognized the cleverness of her personal dress code. White, black, and beige. Nothing, no color, would be permitted to distract from those astounding eyes.

Beside her, Adele Rountree seemed a crude clay copy of a

bone china Dresden figurine. Behind Adele, in lacy jabot, brocaded jacket, and white satin knee breeches, Ham Manville looked foppish enough to justify his choice of costume. Under the lavishly gilt-lace-trimmed tricorne hat and powdered peruke, his face was faintly equine. His eyes were set too closely together, his nose was too long. He resembled, I thought, a slightly less toothy Prince Charles.

They arrived at their table as Nick and Jenny stepped from the dance floor.

"Nickie!" Caroline Manville cawed. "How dashing you look! If I'd known you were going to be Rhett Butler I'd have come as Scarlett O'Hara!"

"Hello, Caroline." Nick tipped his planter's hat. "You look lovely as you are."

"What a charming liar he is." Mrs. Manville directed the comment at Jenny. "I don't believe we've met, my dear. I'm Caroline Manville."

"How do you do." Jenny took the proffered hand. "I'm Jennifer Steele."

"Jennifer Steele!" Adele Rountree, her turquoise eyes wide, snatched Jenny's hand as Caroline released it. "My dear, I'd recognize that voice anywhere. I'm one of your greatest fans!"

"Thank you," Jennifer said faintly. "That's nice to hear."

"Oh, yes. I adored your Amanda. When you left *Halls of Justice* I stopped watching." Adele's voice was breathy and light. "I simply did not enjoy it any longer, you know? Without you, it was just another soap. And to tell the truth, my dear, not a very good one."

"Well . . . I'm sure . . ." Jenny looked down at her hand, firmly engulfed in Adele's.

"Mrs. Rountree?" One of the teenage usherettes appeared at Adele's elbow. "Pardon me for interrupting," she said. "Mr. Jamison sent me to fetch you. There's some trouble about the seating at table twenty-four?"

"Tell him I'll be right there." Adele permitted Jenny to retrieve her hand. "Duty calls," she said brightly. "But I'll see you later, my dear."

She bustled away and the group broke up. Nancy Lee and Ham melted into the crowded dance floor, Caroline Manville joined the Prescotts at their table.

"So. Now you've seen her. What does your gut say?" Nick asked Mike when we were all seated at our table.

"Not much," Mike conceded. "She isn't what I expected."

The band thumped their set's end and Charlie and Larry materialized from the dance floor. Charlie dropped into his chair, heaving a grateful sigh. Larry leaned across him to speak to Jenny.

"I'm going to the car to get my camera," he said.

"You want us to go with you?"

"It's a small camera." Larry smiled. "I think I can manage. I'll be right back."

The lights dimmed a degree and the slow, sensuous beat of "Blue Tango" followed him away. Rafe turned to me.

"This is more my speed, Cat," he said. "Care to dance?"

"I'd love to."

He was a superb dancer, moving fluidly to the music, not talking, leading with such easy grace I lost all sense of time and place. The years fell away and I drifted with the throbbing music, not old, not young, not part of this world or any other. When the band switched to a thumping conga, yanking me back to the present, I felt I'd been away for hours. By mutual consent, Rafe and I left the dance floor.

Charlie, Mike, and Jenny were gathered at one side of the table, their heads together.

"Where's Nick?" I asked, seating myself next to Mike.

"Nancy Lee snatched him," Mike replied.

"Snatched?"

Mike chuckled. "It was beautiful," he said. "She floated over and asked Nick—pardon me, *Nickie*—to dance. It was very obvious Nick wasn't too enthusiastic. A lesser woman would have slunk off, her tail between her legs."

"You had to see it, Cat," Charlie chimed in. "I swear she didn't move a muscle. She just blasted him with those eyes. Believe me, only a man who enjoys kicking puppies could have said no to that face."

"Damn. I always miss everything," I complained.

A white-coated waiter hesitated behind Charlie's chair and asked if we wanted anything from the bar.

Charlie placed our orders and asked, "What about Nick and Larry?"

"Perrier for Nick, white wine for Larry," Jenny said.

"Larry isn't back yet?" I asked of nobody in particular. Nobody answered. Probably nobody heard.

The now-irritating *thump-thump-thump* had brought the conga line to a merciful end, leaving Nick and Nancy Lee at the perimeter of the floor, nearby. I watched, amused, as he quickly dropped his hands from her waist. He grasped her elbow, guided her to her chair, held it until she was seated, and beat a retreat to his seat beside Jenny.

Purely by chance, I was looking at Caroline Manville as she rose from the table, her eyes on Nick, her intent clear. Nick caught her advance from the corner of his eye. He was on his feet instantly, pulling Jenny with him. They vanished into the mob milling to the choppy beat of "Winchester Cathedral."

I had to admire Caroline Manville's élan. She made a quick, slick recovery.

"Well, Charles." Her tone was arch. She looked imperiously at Charlie. "I'd rather hoped you would ask me to dance."

Charlie rose from his chair. "Ah, my dear, I've been waiting for a waltz set to do just that."

"Waltzing's a bore. Why wait?" Caroline slid her hand through Charlie's arm and led him away.

Rafe, watching them go, shook his head sympathetically. "Poor old Charlie," he said. "He'll be limping for a week. Caroline has no more sense of rhythm than a concrete bathtub. I bet anything Nick's danced with her before. Have you ever seen anyone disappear so fast?"

"Speaking of disappearances," I said. "Shouldn't Larry be back by now? Seems to me he's been gone a long time."

"Has he?" Rafe frowned. "Maybe he ran into a friend?"

"Maybe," I conceded, then changed my mind. I stood up. "I think I'll walk up to the car. He's been gone too long."

"I'll go with you," Rafe said. "I need some fresh air."

"I'll go, too." Mike pushed himself up from his chair. "I need a smoke."

We threaded our way through the noisy tables, rode down the escalator, crossed the lobby, and pushed out through the revolving door into the cool, clear night.

"Aaaah." Rafe paused on the stone steps and breathed deeply. "I didn't realize how bad the air was up there."

"Yeah." Mike lit a cigarette, inhaled, and released the smoke contentedly. "Ain't it amazing. Rich people stink just like the rest of us. Tell me something, Rafe, do you and Charlie subject yourselves to evenings like this often?"

"Often enough." Rafe started down the steps.

We followed him and strolled together toward the parking lot, Mike setting a pace comfortable to himself.

"Doesn't look like much fun to me. Does it pay off?"

"You mean do people like the Manvilles buy our antiques? Sometimes. Not as often as you might think. And when they do they're chintzy as hell. People like the Manvilles aren't the customers keeping us in business."

"So why bother?"

"Because when old Auntie Nell dies and her estate goes up for grabs, we're the first dealers they call."

"That's important?"

"That's *all*-important. As old Max puts it, you don't get in first, sonny, you don't get. It's worth a few hours of waltzing arrogant bags like Caroline Manville around to get in first. So we accept it as part of the job. Not the biggest fun part, but what the hell, Mike, nobody gets a one-hundred-percent rose garden guarantee."

"True," Mike agreed. "I guess every trade has its downside. Cat? Isn't that Larry's car up ahead? He's left his trunk open."

We had entered the final dark aisle of the parking lot. Halfway down, the faint glow of a trunk light was reflected on the trunk's upraised door. It was, unmistakeably, Larry's car. My wagon was parked directly next.

I felt an apprehensive twinge. "That's not like Larry," I said. "That car's his baby."

We increased our pace. Rafe hurried ahead. He reached Larry's car while we were several yards back. We heard his horrified, "*Oh, my God,*" then he disappeared from our sight behind the jutting trunk area of a nearer car.

We ran the last few feet.

Larry's harlequin-clad body lay sprawled, his legs under the car, one arm outflung, his head at a grotesque angle.

Rafe, on his knees, looked up at us, his eyes black in the bone-white half-mask.

"He's dead." Rafe's voice was hollow. "He's dead."

24

It doesn't happen the way it does on television. No screaming sirens, no swarming press, no gawking spectators, no yellow tapes marking off the scene of the crime.

Rafe ran back to the hotel and returned with the chief security officer, a stolid, middle-aged man who bent briefly over Larry, eyed us narrowly, and called the police, murmuring inaudibly into his cellular phone.

A squad car arrived almost immediately, followed in minutes by two detectives in a black, unmarked sedan. While one of the detectives questioned Mike and me, sending Rafe back to the hotel to bring out Charlie, Nick, and Jenny, the other talked in low tones with the hotel security man.

An ambulance, only its low beams lit, came and was quickly gone. A tow truck sped away with Larry's silver car. The squad car left, followed by the two detectives, who had taken our names and addresses and told us they would be in contact with us. The parking lot was silent again, dark under the distant stars.

It had all taken not much more than an hour.

25

The doorbell rang at ten-thirty the next morning. *Larry,* was my first thought, as I went to answer. My second thought was, No, not Larry. Not ever again.

It was Mike.

"I've just left Al Rosen," he said, stepping past me into the foyer. "You're not going to like what he told me."

"Who's Al Rosen?" I asked groggily.

"The detective who worked on the Cody mess. Al Rosen. I told you about him." Mike frowned. "You all right, Cat?"

We had separated the night before, Charlie and Rafe to their van, Jenny with Nick, Mike with me, all of us aware of what none of us were willing to say aloud. The attack had been aimed at Jenny. The wrong harlequin had died.

Mike and I had ridden in silence until we reached my house. He had transferred to his own car, told me he would call, and sped away. I had gone to bed, but sleep hadn't come until the small hours and I had overslept.

"I'm okay," I told him, heading for the kitchen. "I just got up a few minutes ago. Coffee should be ready. Come on."

I set out two mugs, poured the freshly brewed coffee, and dropped into the chair across the table from Mike. He took out a pack of cigarettes and lit one. I groaned.

"Oh, hell," I said. "Can I bum one?"

Poker-faced, he pushed the pack across the table.

I took a cigarette, lit it, inhaled, and said, "If I ask for another, don't give it to me." I blew the smoke out in a fragrant stream. "Okay. What is it I'm not going to like?"

"Where's Jenny? Maybe she should hear it, too."

"She didn't come home last night."

Mike's eyebrows lifted but he didn't comment.

"So what did Al Rosen have to say?" I prodded.

"The police are calling it a mugging."

"What!"

"It's not Al's precinct, but he checked into it for me. Apparently there've been several muggings in that parking lot in the last couple of years. A woman was stabbed for her car keys there in July. They took her car. A Porsche."

"Larry wasn't stabbed. His car was still there."

"They think somebody may have driven in or out of the lot and scared the muggers off."

"Do you believe that?"

"Of course I don't. Someone followed Larry from the hotel and killed him, thinking he was Jenny. You know it, I know it."

I shivered. Suddenly, I didn't want the cigarette any longer. I butted it in the ashtray. "How was he killed?"

Mike sighed heavily. "His neck was broken. According to the police report, the trunk lid was brought down on his neck with such force that the larynx, the cervical vertebrae, and the spinal chord were crushed."

"Oh, God." I closed my eyes and saw Larry's face, the fragile skull, the baby-soft blond hair, the slender neck stem . . . I shuddered. "Who. . . . Did you tell Al Rosen? . . . Does he believe . . ."

"I told him everything." Mike's voice was grim. "He said it didn't matter what he believes. What he's hearing is some very iffy speculation about some very prominent people. We don't have photos, we gave them to Morley. No negatives. And we destroyed the other negatives in the box, which may have led somewhere. We have a marriage license, no proof there was never a divorce. What we've got, according to Al, is *bubkes*."

The phone shrilled, startling us both.

I picked it up and a very subdued Charlie said, "Hey, Cat. It's me. How you doing?"

"Not great. How about you?"

"Rotten. Larry's lawyer, Nathan Lewison, just called. He told us Larry had asked to be cremated. There'll be a service for him in the chapel at Leaside Memorial Gardens at eleven Monday morning. Lewison asked us to inform Larry's friends. Do you know of anybody we should call?"

"Other than Jenny and Nick, no. And Mike, of course. He's here now. What about Larry's grandparents?"

"The Woodwards? Lewison is notifying them."

"Sorry, Charlie. I'll tell Jenny and Nick. But I can't think of anybody else."

"You'll be there?"

"We'll be there."

"We'll see you then. Take care."

"You, too, Charlie."

I replaced the phone. It rang immediately. I picked it up and for a moment there was a rushing sound, then Jenny's voice came clear.

"Hello, Cat. It's me." The sound level dipped and I had to strain to hear her next words. "I didn't want to call too early. I didn't wake you, did I?"

"No. I was up. Where are you? We don't seem to have a very good connection."

"I'm on Nick's car phone. We just went through a tunnel. Can you hear me now?"

"Perfectly. Are you all right?"

"I'm okay. We're going to Nick's country place for the weekend. Do you mind?"

"For goodness sake, Jenny, why would I mind?" I repeated Charlie's information and asked, "Will you be back in time?"

"Just a minute." I listened to a muffled drone, then Jenny returned. "We'll be back early Monday morning. Nick says about seven. He has a court appearance at nine but he thinks he'll be through well before eleven. We can all go to the . . . the service together."

"Good. Jenny?" I hesitated about giving useless advice, then went ahead anyway. "Try to put everything out of your mind until Monday. Drift. Take in the autumn colors, look at the sky, listen to the birds. Just drift for the weekend."

"I'll try," she said, then added softly, "Cat? I love you."

I listened to the dial tone for three startled seconds, then hung up the phone. Mike was watching me with raised eyebrows. "So?" he asked.

"Did you know Nick had a country house? They're on their way there. For the weekend."

Mike nodded. "She'll be safe with Nick."

"Safe? You think they're going to try again?"

"I don't know." Mike rose from the table. "That was good advice you gave Jenny. Let's go look at some sky."

We drove country roads, to a town named Valleyfield, and stopped for lunch at a small café Mike knew where they served homemade soup and dessert, then took a longer route home.

"What are you going to do tomorrow?" Mike asked when I parked in the driveway.

"I don't know. If it's nice, I'll rake leaves and dig up the dahlia bulbs. If it rains, I'll probably bake."

"Bake?"

"Turn on some music, get out the flour, grease some pans, and bake up a storm. World's best therapy."

"If you say so." Mike unlocked the door to his own car and slid behind the wheel. "G'night, Cat. See you Monday."

As it turned out, I did both gardening and baking on Sunday. I finished raking the front lawn and had the leaves bagged before the sky began spitting a cold rain.

I went into my warm house, chose Nana Mouskouri to bake with, and turned out two dozen banana muffins, a sour-cream coffee cake, and an apple cake. Plus a quiche for my supper.

I crawled into bed at ten, too deliciously weary to think, and fell asleep immediately.

26

Nick dropped Jenny off shortly after eight in the morning. He waved from the car and sped away.

"We forgot to set the alarm," Jenny explained. "He's got less than an hour to get home, change his clothes, and show up in court."

She wore a large, white knit fisherman's sweater, the sleeves rolled back, and black corduroy pants with turned-up cuffs. On her feet were the bronze ballet slippers she had worn Friday night.

"Have you had breakfast?" I asked.

"Haven't eaten, haven't showered, haven't even brushed my teeth," she said. "Out of bed, into the car, *zoom.*"

"Are you hungry? Or would you rather shower first?"

"I'm starving. But if it's okay with you, I'd like to have a shower first. I feel grungy."

"Go ahead. I'm making apple pancakes."

She was back in the kitchen ten minutes later, wearing my terry robe, a towel wrapped around her head. She crossed to the garbage pail, raised the lid, and dropped the bronze slippers into the pail.

"You're throwing them out?" I asked. Stupid question.

She let the lid fall with a thud. "I burned the costume in Nick's fireplace. I never want to see it again. I can't stop thinking it was me they were after, that if Larry had been wearing some other outfit, he'd still be alive."

"Maybe, maybe not. The police think he was killed by parking lot muggers."

"Muggers?" Jenny said blankly. "Larry was *mugged?*"

"That's what they told Mike."

"Do you believe them? Does Mike?"

The phone rang before I had to decide whether to lie to her or not. I picked it up. An unfamiliar male voice asked to speak to Jenny.

"One moment, please." I held out the phone. "For you."

She took the phone and I went back to the stove to pour batter over the sautéed apple slices.

Jenny said hello, then listened, leaning on the counter, the phone pressed to her ear.

"Not until this afternoon," she said moments later. "Fine. Four-thirty's fine." Pause. "Okay, g'bye, Matt."

She replaced the phone in its cradle and turned to me, her face a mixture of emotions. "That was Matt," she said in a strange and wondering voice.

"What's wrong?"

"Nothing's wrong." Jenny shook her head. The towel she had wrapped around her hair unwound and fell across her face. She dropped it on the counter and sat down at the table, a bemused smile on her face. "Crazy," she said.

"Wait." I flipped the pancakes onto a platter, picked up the coffee percolator on my way to the table, and sat down across from her. "Okay. Go."

"All those years." She gazed down at the pancakes on her plate. "If you knew, Cat. All the cattle calls, the kissing up to casting directors, the begging for parts, all those years of getting a part, doing the best job you know how and a damn good job too, and when it's over, back to square one. All those years. And, in the end, all it really takes is a roll of the dice."

I waited. "Jenny," I finally said, impatiently.

She looked up at me, startled, then she giggled, the snuffling giggle I remembered from her teenage years. I couldn't help smiling at the memory.

"It's crazy!" She laughed out loud this time. "*Halls of Justice* wants to write me back into the show. I didn't die, see, somebody else did—do you believe it? I'm the cover story this week on two national rags. A production company wants to buy my story for a TV movie. Matt says he has me lined up for three national talk shows. Cameo roles on umpteen TV sit-coms and series if I want. It's crazy."

The laughter faded suddenly. "You know what it is?" she said to her plate. "It's the shits. I worked so damn hard for so damn long to get practically nowhere. And all I really had to do was lose my mind for a year."

"Hey. Jenny." I leaned across the table and lifted her chin so she had to look into my eyes. "You take it any way you can get it. Even lame gift horses are few and far between."

She grimaced and relaxed. "You're right," she said and took my hand in hers. "You know what? I miss Larry. I wish he was here. He'd have gone ape over all this."

"Wouldn't he though." I withdrew my hand and began to eat. "He'd have rushed off and bought a white mink coat and a diamond tiara."

Jenny grinned. "For him or for me?"

"Both. Eat, Jenny. We have to get moving."

27

There were no headstones at Leaside Memorial Gardens. Brass plaques were set flush into clipped lawns in areas divided by flower beds, shrub groupings, and graceful trees under which white wrought-iron benches had been placed. A placid stream wended its way, ending in a large pond that reflected the sky and the willows surrounding it.

The chapel was a small fieldstone building, set in a grove of cedars. I recognized Charlie and Rafe's van, parked behind Mike's car. I pulled in behind an unfamiliar navy blue car and Jenny and I walked the curving flagstone path to the oaken doors.

Inside, a center aisle led between oak benches to a raised dais. There was no denominational insignia in the room, only a large and beautiful stained-glass rose window filtering light down on an unadorned oak pulpit.

Mike, Charlie, and Rafe were near the pulpit, talking in low tones to a lean, balding, middle-aged man wearing heavy horn-rimmed glasses and a brown suit. Charlie introduced us. He was Nathan Lewison, Larry's lawyer.

Simultaneously, a clock began chiming the hour, soft guitar music seeped from hidden speakers, a very tall woman in a severe black suit entered through a door beneath the rose window, and Nick came striding down the aisle.

The woman in black positioned herself behind the pulpit and waited out the clock with bent head and downcast eyes. When the final note sounded, she raised her head and gestured with pale, bony hands.

"We who have come to mourn our friend will join together in our sorrow." She spoke in a funereal monotone. "We will form a loving circle and we will mourn as one."

When we had arranged ourselves to her satisfaction, she reached down, withdrew a small, white satin pillow and placed it on the pulpit.

"We have come to say good-bye to our friend, Lawrence Woodward Mendelsohn," she said. Reaching under the pulpit once more, she produced a single, long-stemmed white rose.

"Good night, sweet Prince." She placed the rose on the pillow. "And flights of angels sing thee to thy rest."

She paused long enough for me to wonder, *that's it?* Then she continued in that irritatingly sepulchral voice. "We will each say good-bye in our own way," she said. "I will begin."

She raised soulful eyes and gazed over our heads.

"Lawrence was a child of the universe, even as we are," she intoned. "His time with us was short. He was taken from us too soon. He has left a gap in our lives that can never be filled. We shall miss him. We shall remember him."

I glanced across the circle at Mike. He raised mocking brows and I looked away quickly to avoid the embarrassment of a snicker. His thoughts may as well have been printed on his forehead: *What's with all the us and we? This bimbo didn't even know him.*

She reached out and grasped Charlie's right hand. "Will you speak of our friend," she said. It was not a question.

Charlie looked around, startled. Realizing there was no graceful way out, he began, "Uh. Yeah. Larry."

His one visible eyebrow drew down. "There used to be a singer named Hoagy Carmichael. He wrote a song he called 'Hong Kong Blues.' There's one line in it, 'I need someone to love me,' and Hoagy always dragged out the *neeeed*, in that croaky voice he had. To me, that line was Larry. We never told you, Larry. But we did love you. So long, kid."

That did it. My eyes prickled, my throat thickened. I wouldn't be able to say a word.

"Take the hand of the friend next to you," the woman instructed. Charlie, somewhat abashed, took Mike's hand.

"Speak," she commanded.

Mike's eyes flew wide, then he began to quiver with suppressed laughter. He shook his head, reached for Rafe's hand. Rafe, muttering something unintelligible, grabbed my hand. I didn't even attempt to say anything.

Nick and Jenny and Nathan Lewison all passed. When we were joined, holding hands, the woman swept us with a look of sheer loathing.

"Farewell, Lawrence Woodward Mendelsohn," she spat. She turned and marched stiffly out the door through which she had come. The door eased shut behind her.

For a moment there was silence, then Mike spoke, softly menacing.

"Cat, if you pull a mail-order funeral like this on me, I swear I'll come back and haunt you. I want a party. I want booze and food and loud music. Then I want you to take my ashes and dump me in a strawberry field somewhere. You promise?"

"I promise. Let's get out of here."

"One minute," Nick said. "I've arranged lunch for us at the Capri. I hope all of you can come."

Only Nathan Lewison demurred, pleading a previous lunch meeting with a client.

"All right." Nick took Jenny's arm. "Suppose we all meet at the Capri, then."

28

Nick had reserved one of the private dining rooms upstairs for us. A lavish buffet had been set up on a sideboard. A large round table, covered with snowy linen, was surrounded by eight high-backed chairs, upholstered in a rich, cobalt velvet.

Jenny stood in front of the sideboard, an empty plate in her hand, a helpless expression on her face.

"It looks so good and it smells so good," she said. "And I don't think I can eat a thing."

"Yes, you can." I took the plate from her and selected from the buffet. "You've a couple of rough days ahead, Jenny. You're going to have to remember to eat regularly."

"What rough days?" Mike frowned.

Jenny sat down at the table beside him. "I'm going to New York for a couple of days," she said. She picked at her Caesar salad.

Mike's frown deepened. "You're going to New York? Who's going with you?"

"Nobody's going with me. Why?"

"I don't like the idea of your going alone," Mike said. "The first time, Larry was with you. Then Nick. I don't think you should be going alone."

Jenny set her fork down carefully. She looked at Mike. "You don't believe Larry was mugged."

"Of course I don't. Nor does anyone else." He fanned a hand to include the rest of us at the table. "That's why you shouldn't be going alone."

"Dammit." Jenny's cheeks were suddenly pink. She pushed her chair back and rose angrily to her feet. "*Goddammit. I* won't live like this. What the hell are the police doing? Why hasn't somebody been arrested?"

"Like who?" Mike asked reasonably. "Nancy Lee? Morley? The hairy René? Or somebody we don't even know about from the negatives we destroyed?"

"I don't know, goddammit!" Jenny snarled. "But I know for goddamn sure I can't hide here and wait. If I don't grab what's going for me right now, I'm last week's news. There has to be some way to find out who."

"Sure." Mike shrugged at her, smiling. "We can run an ad. Anyone interested in taking a shot at Jennifer Steele, apply in writing to box number *oh, oh.*"

"Dammit, Mike, that's not funny."

"Of course it's not. But a tantrum isn't going to do it, either. Sit down, Jenny. Use your head. Look. We know someone is after you. We just don't know who. Maybe we can find a way of bringing them out into the open."

"Why not just hang a rope around my neck and tie me to a stake? Isn't that what they do with goats? Live bait?"

"Hey! That might work." Mike grinned at her.

Jenny laughed, her anger dissipated. She punched his shoulder, not gently. "You bastard," she said. She picked up her fork and stabbed at her salad.

"I think I might have an idea," Rafe said quietly. All eyes turned on him. He shrugged. "It may not work. But it's worth a try."

"Don't get humble on us," Charlie said. "Tell."

"We're doing an antique show this weekend," Rafe said. "Friday and Saturday. The admission fee and ten percent of the dealer's sales go to the Sick Children's Hospital."

"Rafe." Charlie grimaced. "Nobody cares about all that crap. What's your idea?"

"Just background, Charlie." Rafe glanced around at the rest of us. "Maybe you know that Barbra Streisand sold off her art deco collection? My idea is for Jennifer Steele to sell off her art nouveau collection."

"My *what* collection?" Jenny asked blankly.

"I don't get it," Charlie said.

"Go on, Rafe." Nick leaned forward, his face sharp, his eyes an intense green. "A personal appearance?"

Rafe nodded. "We run an ad. Canterbury House is selling off the Steele collection at the Tudor Hotel Antique Show. Jennifer Steele will be present from, say, two o'clock until four, on Friday. We can throw in, somehow, that she's moving to Los Angeles, this will be the last opportunity to see her in person? Maybe some *bumpf* about having her sign the pieces that are sold?"

Charlie frowned. "You honestly think someone's going to try to get to her at an antique show?"

"Hell, I don't know, Charlie. If they figure it's their last chance at her? Maybe. We'll see what turns up."

"Rafe," I said. "By Friday she'll be on the covers of the supermarket scandal rags. Plus a couple of national talk shows. What turns up could be a bunch of curiosity seekers wanting to get a look at her."

"At twenty-five bucks a crack? The admission price to the show should keep out the riffraff." Rafe eyed the dubious faces surrounding him. He threw up his hands. "All right. So it's a lousy idea."

Mike had been listening with narrowed, musing eyes. He tilted his head. "Kitty Drummond," he said. "Hell, we don't take out an ad. We get Kitty to run a puff piece. She can put in all the crap about the last chance our fair city will have to see Jennifer in person, and take in the fabulous Steele art nouveau collection, all at the same time."

"Listen, you guys," Jenny intervened. "Would somebody please tell me what the hell an art nouveau collection is?"

"Don't worry, sweetie pie." Charlie, accepting the idea as a possibility, was suddenly enthusiastic. "We'll put a collection together that'll knock your socks off. What've we got, Rafe? The Tiffany Studios lamp? The Charpentier mantel clock! The WMF punch bowl. What else, what else?"

"The Horta mirror. The Ferez screen," Rafe added. "The Loetz vase. And the Daum. The Gorham sterling. The bronze andirons. We can put together enough pieces to count as a collection. The Boverie lemon-wood desk. Old Mrs. Van-Scoy's cameos. The *plique-à-jour* dragonfly pin. The Gallé and the Majorelle you stripped, Cat."

"Sounds good," I said. "There's only one thing that worries me. Will Jenny be in any real danger?"

"I don't see how," Charlie assured me. "Rafe and I will both be right there."

"Charlie," I said, worried, "you're there to sell. Suppose you get swamped with customers? Suppose gobs of celebrity gawkers show? Or media people? You can't watch everybody."

"Cat's got a point." Mike frowned. "Is there room for five in your booth? She and I could keep an eye on Jenny."

"That won't work." Rafe shook his head. "Five of us standing around? For one thing, there isn't the space. For another, it would look unnatural. You could pass as customers for a few minutes, not for two solid hours."

"What about the dealers around you? Maybe we could hang out with one for a while, then move on to another."

"We have a corner booth. There's only the booth directly across and the one to our right."

"Who are they? Do you know who they are?"

"We have the booth designations back at the shop," Rafe said. "We'll check out our neighbors as soon as we get back and give you a call. If they're friendly types, we'll talk to them for you."

"Good enough," Mike agreed. He turned to Jenny, beside him. "Will you be back Friday?"

"As far as I know, I'll be back Thursday."

"Fine. Then it's up to you. Do we or don't we?"

Jenny shrugged. "It's probably the only way I'll ever find out what an art nouveau collection is. Let's do it."

29

Charlie called as I was preparing dinner for Mike and myself.

"Albion Antiques have the booth facing us," he said. "Ros and Mike Hennessy."

"Great. I know them. Who's beside you?"

"Chapter and Verse. Antique books. Danny Garrette."

"Hey, terrific. I know Danny, too. Haven't seen him for ages. We did a flea market, side by side, one summer."

"Dan did flea markets?" Charlie was surprised. "I didn't know that. He has a shop, *très élégant.* You want me to phone them or will you?"

"I'll call."

"Okay, you call. But don't go 'way. I have an absolutely gorgeous what-goes-around-comes-around story for you. Nathan Lewison came to see us."

"Larry's lawyer?"

"Larry's lawyer. He had a few of Larry's *tchotchkes* he thought we might be interested in having and he told us the story. You'll love it, Cat. Are you ready for this?"

"I'm ready."

"A year or so ago, Larry bought a bed-and-breakfast place, just outside Sutton Village, near the lake."

"A bed-and-breakfast? What on earth did Larry want . . ."

"Don't interrupt. He bought it. Nathan said it's one of those big old places, twenty rooms, gables, porch all around. It's situated on the only road into the lake, right where the road parts to go left and right, around the lake. No lake frontage, but it has a swimming pool. Larry paid more than a quarter of a mil for it."

"Bed-and-breakfast?" I said, mystified. "Larry?"

"It seems Larry had convinced himself he was going to die of AIDS, probably sooner than later. He began renovations for the Nora Woodward Mendelsohn Retreat House. Great big shiny brass plaque on the gates."

"Nora Woodward. His mother."

"Right. It's a last refuge house for gay men dying of AIDS. *Only* gay men. Financed by the five million bucks she left Larry. It opens this coming spring."

"Five million? Larry had five million dollars?"

"More. But that isn't the exquisite part," Charlie said. "The Woodwards have a cottage on the lake that's been in the family for several generations. A showplace, apparently. Remember, Cat, there's only the one road in. The Woodwards are going to have to pass by this gay leper colony—*with their daughter's name on it*—every time they drive into or away from the ancestral shack. And there isn't one damn thing they can do about it. This *Jew-fag* grandson of theirs found a way of giving them the permanent finger. With Woodward money, Cat. Ain't it luverly?"

"It's positively Machiavellian," I said faintly. "Did Larry plan . . ."

"Every inch of the way," Charlie said. "Nathan told us Larry specified it was to be that house and no other. He paid twenty thousand more than the place was worth to get it."

"Larry . . ." I began. Gentle, accommodating Larry? "It's hard to . . . I guess I didn't know him very well."

"I know what you mean," Charlie said. "The only one who isn't surprised is Rafe. And that's because he has the same dark and devious Mediterranean mind. *Hey!*"

I heard the sounds of a scuffle, Rafe's voice, Charlie's laughter, then Rafe came on the phone.

"Hi, Cat," he said. "We're putting Jenny's collection together. It's looking very impressive. Has Mike talked to Kitty Drummond yet?"

"Yes, and she'll cooperate. Mike said she loves it. He's meeting her tomorrow with the details. She promised it for Thursday's paper."

Mike waved from the kitchen table. "Ask Rafe if he'll make a list. I'll pick it up on the way."

I relayed the message. Rafe said the list would be ready and added, "If anything comes up, we'll call. Otherwise we'll see you on Friday."

"With Jenny. At two o'clock. We'll be there."

30

Jenny phoned Thursday night to tell me she wouldn't be returning until the next morning. So on Friday, at twelve-forty-five, I was waiting for her plane, which landed forty-five minutes late.

I caught sight of her striding down the ramp, and felt a sudden odd sense of detachment, as if I was watching the approach of a personality from the newspaper pages, not someone I knew.

She was wearing a flaring camel-colored cape over a cream sweater. Her skirt was finely pleated, printed in autumn shades, and reached to the tops of her shiny tan boots. Her hair was dressed in that stringy, unbrushed style I'll never appreciate.

She walked very quickly, her eyes searching ahead. Heads craned as she passed and I heard someone nearby say, "Isn't that Jennifer Steele?"

With scarcely a break in stride she hooked her hand through my arm and pulled me along.

"Keep walking," she muttered. "If we stop, it'll take ages to get away."

I was out of breath when we reached my car. She slid into the passenger seat, fastened her seat belt, and gave me a wide smile. "Fun, eh?" she asked.

"Hell, yes," I panted. "So much fun we forgot your bags."

"No bags. I'm going back tonight."

"Tonight?" I started the car and backed out. "Why do you have to go back tonight?"

"Tomorrow starts early. We're shooting promos at six in the morning. I've signed for two weeks on *Halls of Justice*, after which they'll kill me off again, I suppose. After that, I'm off to the coast to do a TV series pilot. And then a movie, *Return to Singapore*. Shooting starts in December."

"That's great." I glanced at her, expecting to see her elated. She was frowning down at her clasped hands. "What's the matter, Jenny? Aren't you pleased?"

"Yes. Of course, I'm pleased." She was silent a moment. "I was just thinking about Larry," she said. "He always wanted to see Singapore."

I risked a second glance. A small, wistful smile lay softly on her lips.

"He had a tour all planned. He'd fly around the world and stop off in cities he thought were romantic. He loved names like Shanghai, Casablanca, Mandalay, where the flying fishes play, Monterrey, Sorrento."

The smile faded.

"He'll never see them now." Her voice was low. The words came out painfully. "I'm the one who should be dead and I'll see Singapore."

"Jenny . . ." I began, but I couldn't find the right words. I pulled up to the parking attendant's booth and handed over the ticket and money.

Once into the traffic stream, I asked her if she had told Nick her news. There was no answer.

"I'm sorry, Jen," I apologized. "It's none of my business."

"No," Jenny said. "That's not it, Cat."

Cat? I wondered when she had stopped calling me Catherine. I hadn't noticed.

We rode in silence for almost a mile, then she said, "I know this is going to sound like a schlock movie . . ."

I drove, waiting for her to continue.

"When I'm with Nick," she said finally, "it's as if we've known . . . oh, shit, this is going to sound so dumb . . . as if our flesh has known another life together, a life before this one. It's like a thirst, until we touch, you know? But that's all there is, there ain't no more."

"What do you mean?"

"I mean, that's what there is between us. That's *all* there is between us. And it isn't enough. Nick won't, or maybe he can't, ever let anyone get close. And I've worked too hard and waited too long to throw it all away over an attack of galloping hormones."

My thruway exit was approaching and I concentrated on getting into the right-hand lane. Once there, I asked, "Does Nick know you're going?"

"He knows. I called him last night."

"How does he feel about it?"

Jenny laughed, somehow a sad sound. "Cat, I don't believe anyone, anytime, anywhere will ever know how Nick Kramer feels about anything."

I took the exit ramp and we drove the two blocks to the hotel without speaking. A parking lot attendant replaced me at the wheel and we entered the hotel.

Passing by the newsstand, I saw Jenny's face smiling out at us from the covers of two publications and I watched as heads turned to follow her swift and purposeful progress across the lobby to the escalators rising to the mezzanine floor. She stepped onto the escalator and turned to face me on the step behind.

"Quick," she said. "What's an art nouveau collection?"

"It's a collection from the art nouveau period, starting somewhere in the eighteen nineties and extending to the early nineteen hundreds. Furniture, glass, paintings, jewelry, metal articles, all kinds of things. Lovely stuff."

"And what was it that Barbra Streisand collected? Art something else."

"Deco. Art deco. It's an art style that began at the Paris International Exhibition in nineteen twenty-five. Went on through the thirties and early forties. I don't like it. You might."

"If you don't, I don't. Why do I like art nouveau?"

"Uh . . . fluid lines, graceful, natural forms. Ladies with long flowing hair in long flowing robes. You can say you began your collection after you saw a Mucha poster."

"A *what* poster?"

"Mucha." I spelled it for her. "Alphonse Mucha." We had almost reached the mezzanine. "Forget the Alphonse. Just say you were inspired by Mucha."

"Mucha." She grinned down at me. "Gotcha."

She turned and a sudden brilliant flash of light lit up her halo of hair. For a split second, before I realized it was a camera flash, I felt a stab of real fear.

Jenny stepped from the escalator and was immediately surrounded by a milling horde of media people. Actually, there couldn't have been more than eight or ten of them, but their jockeying for position and their shouting of questions was overpowering. I was pushed aside and lost sight of Jenny for a moment. Then Charlie was there, taking over by force of size and sheer presence.

"Let her breathe, kids," he roared genially. "Give her some space. You'll get your stories and all the pictures you want inside."

With one arm around Jenny, using the other to clear a way ahead, Charlie made progress across the lobby toward the ballroom where the show had been set up. I trailed in his wake, staying close.

"Yo, Jennifer," a chubby man with a magnificent walrus mustache called out, "how did you survive on the street?"

Jenny flashed a smile at him. "One day at a time!"

"Why did you start collecting art nouveau, Miss Steele?" The question came from an artsy-looking woman whose snowy hair was cut in a severe Dutch-boy bob. "When did you start?"

"I started years ago." Jenny beamed. "After I saw my first Mucha poster. I love the flowing lines and graceful, natural forms, don't you?"

I smiled to myself. Jenny had always been a quick study.

"Why are you selling?" The woman persisted.

"I need the money!" Jenny called back over her shoulder as we stepped through the entrance into the ballroom.

I detached myself from Charlie's heels and followed at a more comfortable distance. The media group had been increased by curious onlookers. By the time we reached the

Canterbury House booth, it was impossible for me to get close. I scanned the crowd, searching for Mike and found him in the Chapter and Verse booth with Danny Garrette, both watching me with wide grins on their faces.

"Hey, Cat," Danny called. "Come on in here before you get stomped on."

Danny is one of my favorite people in the world of collectors. He's a gentle, literate man in his early fifties, with dark, humorous eyes, a black mustache, and a fund of stories from a peripatetic life. He's been, among other things, an editor for the *New York Times*, a hotel clerk in Jerusalem, a newspaper reporter in New Mexico, an eviscerator on a Long Island chicken farm, and a gas station jockey in the Canadian Rockies. The summer we spent with adjoining stalls at an outdoor flea market we talked and laughed a lot more than we sold.

I circled his main display table and hugged him.

"Great to see you, Danny." I looked from Dan to Mike. "You two know each other?"

"We knew each other when. . . ." Danny smiled.

"When what?"

"When Danny was entertainment editor on the *Star*," Mike said. "I lost track of him after the paper folded. We've been playing catch-up for the last half hour."

"Mike filled me in on Jenny's story," Danny said. "That was quite an entrance your bag lady just made. I assume our vigil begins now? Who do we watch?"

"Anybody who gets too close," Mike answered. His gaze swivelled past and around me. "Morley Richards and the hairy René are here somewhere, Cat," he said. "And I saw Julian Shaw a couple of minutes ago."

"Julian Shaw?"

"One of the filthy-picture boys. The judge, remember? He's the one Morley said was in Spain last November."

"Oh, yes. I remember. Have you seen the Manvilles?"

"Caroline Manville was at my table earlier," Danny said. "She was with Mrs. Adele Rountree."

"Adele Rountree? You know her?"

Danny nodded. "I bought the Rountree–Quincy library

after the old boy disposed of himself." He grinned. "Adele got decidedly pissy when she saw the price I've put on her great-grandaddy's eighteen fifty-four edition of Lempriere's classical dictionary."

"Poor baby." The crowd was thinning in front of the Canterbury House booth, the media people drifting away. I could see the Albion Antiques display, directly across from Charlie and Rafe, and Ros Hennessy in her wheelchair behind the table. She looked up, her pretty face broke into a smile, and she waved.

Danny moved away to serve a customer.

"Why don't you stay with Danny, Mike? I'll go over and park myself with Ros and Mike Hennessy."

"Sounds good." Mike nodded.

I stopped to ask Rafe if he had spoken to Morley about the negatives René Junot had been so determined to have.

"I called him several times during the week," Rafe said. "All I got was his answering machine."

"He's here. With Junot."

"We'll watch for them," Rafe promised.

"How's it going?"

"Good. The Gallé's gone. Also the Boverie desk, the Daum vase, and the Larch inkwell."

"Terrific. You haven't seen Nancy Lee, have you?"

"Not so far." Rafe's constantly roving eye paused. He touched my arm. "Excuse me, Cat. Customer."

I crossed the aisle to Albion Antiques.

"And about time, Cat." Ros greeted me in her soft Sussex burr. "You piqued our curiosity with your phone call. Now you must sit down and give us all the gory details."

Rosalynde Hennessy is the only British woman I've ever met whose voice pitch and diction don't set my teeth on edge. She has a dulcet, Home Counties accent and her voice is low and soft. A type of muscular dystrophy that confines her to a wheelchair has done nothing to curb an irreverent sense of humor. Mike Hennessy is a big Irishman with an untamed red beard, wicked blue eyes, a hollow leg, and a sly, iconoclastic soul. And one of the dirtiest laughs I've ever heard.

Between serving customers and wrapping and bagging their purchases, it was almost an hour before they had the full story. By then, all the coffee I'd sucked up, waiting for Jenny's plane, was demanding an outlet.

"There's a posh restroom down at the other end of the ballroom." Ros waved her hand to the left. "But if all you need is a simple whiz, there's a loo the vendors are using. It's behind Danny's stall, just down the hall a piece."

When I returned, an influx of antique hunters and the curious had filled the aisles. The big room was ahum with well-bred murmuring and stirring and it wasn't until I had slipped behind Ros's display table that I saw Nancy Lee.

She was inspecting a set of sterling silver figural napkin rings, the last thing I'd have guessed would interest her. She was wearing a deceptively simple beige knit dress and a long string of matched pearls. Her pale gold hair had been drawn back in a loose French braid.

I bent over Ros. "That's Nancy Lee, the woman Mike's serving," I muttered.

"Oh my," Roz murmured.

Nancy Lee touched her bottom lip doubtfully. "You really think they're an appropriate wedding gift?" she asked in her breathy, small voice.

"They'll become family heirlooms," Mike assured her.

"What a lovely thought." Nancy Lee produced her wallet and extracted a credit card. "I'll take them."

"Oh my, those eyes." Ros marvelled as Nancy Lee drifted across the aisle with her purchase.

"Contact lenses," Mike snorted.

"Nope. They're for real," I said. "Her mother has them, too. They're Quincy eyes, don't you know."

"Sounds like something you spread on toast," Mike said.

"Gah." Ros wrinkled her nose. "Do we watch her?"

"But not too obviously. We can't, all of us, be standing around, staring holes into her."

"Don't be silly, Cat." Ros smiled. "When somebody looks like that, staring is de riguer. Stare away. That woman is accustomed to being gawked at."

I watched Nancy Lee with a growing sense of unease. She had passed by Jenny without a glance and stopped to inspect the Horta wall mirror. It wasn't until she placed her hand on the sleeve of Charlie's black-velvet jacket that I realized what was bothering me.

The hand was small and very slender. *She* was small and very slender, a full twelve inches shorter than Charlie. Soaking wet, she wouldn't weigh more than a hundred pounds. It would have taken a very much taller, much stronger, and much heavier individual to reach beyond Larry, who must have been bent over the open trunk, grasp the lid, and bring it down with enough force to break his neck.

"I'll be back," I told Ros, and crossed the aisle.

Rafe listened to my doubts, frowning, his eye measuring Nancy Lee.

"You've got a point, Cat," he agreed. "I could visualize her stabbing Cody after she'd coldcocked him from behind. Or running Jenny down with a car. But I think you're right. She just doesn't look physically capable of killing Larry. Not the way it was done."

"Morley and René are both big men. And Mike saw Julian Shaw earlier. Have they been around?"

"Nope. Haven't seen hide nor hair of any of them. Looks like we bombed." Rafe shrugged. "Well, what the hell, it was an idea."

"And a good one. Even if it didn't pay off."

Rafe smiled. "Oh, it paid off. Although not the way we hoped. Canterbury House got a lot of free publicity and we sold several pieces we might not have sold otherwise." He glanced at his watch. "It's getting close to four o'clock, Cat. I think we'd better rescue Jenny."

Jenny, surrounded again, was signing autographs for a sextet of twittering matrons, all with beige-dyed hair, all wearing a variation of the Chanel suit and pearls. I sidled into the group and hissed, "Jenny!"

Jenny nodded to me and smiled dazzlingly at her soap opera fan club. "Please." She looked at each of them in turn. "Would you all excuse me for just a moment?"

We withdrew a few feet and I murmured, "Can you break it up? It's almost four."

"Give me a couple of minutes." Maintaining her radiant smile, Jenny added, "Cat? Do you have an aspirin? I've got a hell of a headache."

"I don't have any. But there's probably a vending machine in the ladies' room. I'll bring you some."

"I'll meet you there. I'm also in urgent need of a pee."

"Okay. It's down the hall, just behind Danny's booth."

"Two minutes."

Jenny returned to being charming. I trotted down the hall and pushed open the door to the ladies' room.

There were no vending machines on the mirrored left-hand wall. On the right, beyond the three toilet stalls, was an alcove with two sinks, a trash bin, and three wall dispensers, one with Certs, one with Sheiks, and one with Tylenol, which struck me as an appropriate before, during, and after selection for casual encounters of the libidinous kind.

There were only two quarters in my change purse and the Tylenol dispenser demanded four. In the depths of my handbag I found enough dimes and nickles to make up the dollar and shoved them all into the vending machine. The machine spat before I was prepared and the small, plastic vial hit the floor, rolling.

Damn. I had no more change. There was nothing to be done but get down on my knees and find the stupid vial.

It had rolled into the nearest stall and come to rest against the toilet bowl base. I flattened out, extended my arm, and had just grasped it when the door to the restroom *whooshed* open and Jenny's shiny tan boots clicked on the ceramic tile floor. She was barely into the room when the door flew open again.

From my almost prone position on the floor I could see it all reflected in the wall mirror. Jenny, walking toward the alcove. Behind her, Adele Rountree, her arm upraised. In her hand, a knife with a long, shiny blade. I could see it. But for two clicks, I could not accept what my eyes were telling me was true. Then I screamed.

"*Jenny! Look out!*"

What happened then was as measured and precise as a ballet. One, two, three.

Adele Rountree lunged forward.

Jenny leaped aside.

I grabbed Adele's right ankle with both hands and yanked as hard as I could.

Adele staggered back, off balance but still erect.

I scrambled to my feet. "Get in here!" I shrieked at Jenny. "*Get in here!*"

She squeezed into the stall, past me. I slammed the metal door and dropped the lock into place.

"Is she crazy?" Jenny was wild-eyed. "Did you see that knife? Is she out of her mind? *Cat! Look out!*"

I jumped away from the door just as Adele's arm swept in an arc across the floor, the knife missing my shoe by a hair. Then her face was there, Quincy eyes glaring, as she began slithering on her stomach under the stall door.

"*Stop it!*" Jenny screamed at her. "Are you crazy? Get away, you crazy old woman!"

Adele Rountree didn't look crazy to me. What she looked was single-mindedly determined to destroy Jenny if she had to crawl on her belly to do it. What was even more frightening than her fixation was her silence. Other than panting with effort, she hadn't made a sound.

She was in to her waist, knife arm swinging, long knife slashing, pressing us back. We clambered up onto the toilet seat, clinging together, and stared helplessly down into that distorted face. Unless we could smother her in toilet paper, there seemed to be no way we could stop her.

Suddenly there was a *whoosh*, a pounding of feet, a loud *whack!*, and she disappeared, her head striking the bottom of the door, her arms flailing along the floor. We heard the sound of scuffling, then Mike's voice.

"Okay, kids," he called. "You can come out now."

We helped each other step down from the toilet seat, both on trembling legs, and opened the stall door.

Adele Rountree lay facedown, her legs kicking futilely.

Mike sat on one of her outflung arms, Mike Hennessy on the other. Danny sat on her back, legs straddling her shoulders, a large book clasped in his arms. The knife had been kicked to the far wall.

"Jesus, oh, Jesus. Thank you, God," Jenny said shakily. "I've never been so scared in my life. That woman is nuts."

"Where did you guys come from?" I looked down at three grinning faces. "How did you know?"

"Ros," Mike Hennessy said. "She was on her way to the can and saw this bag of shit sneaking down the hall after Jenny."

"Didn't Adele see Ros?"

"Cat, you'd be surprised how often people in wheelchairs are invisible. Sure, she saw her. Looked right at her. That's how Ros twigged. The Quincy eyes. So she does a one-eighty degree turn, scoots back to get us, and we come roaring down and there's this massive ass about to slide away under the door. Danny gives her one hell of a whack on the butt with his book, Mike and I each grab a leg and yank her out like a rotten tooth. So here we are, ain't we got fun?"

I frowned down at Danny. "You brought a *book?*"

"I just sort of automatically grabbed the only weapon at hand," Danny explained, somewhat sheepishly. "Weird, huh?"

"Not so weird," Mike Melnyk chortled. "Working on the principle that the pen is mightier than the sword, it makes a certain sense."

"Jesus Murphy." Jenny shook her head. "A bunch of clowns." She poked Adele's thigh with the toe of her boot. "So what happens now? You're not planning on letting this maniac loose, are you?"

"Ros was alerting hotel security," Mike Hennessy assured her. "They should be here any minute."

Adele, who had stopped kicking and turned herself into an inert mass of flesh, suddenly came to life. Bucking like a steer, she almost unseated Danny. She twisted her head and bit into his ankle.

"Dammit." Danny thumped his book down on her head

and snatched his foot away. "Mrs. Rountree," he protested mildly, "that was not a nice thing to do."

"Not *nice?*" Jenny began to laugh, a trace of hysteria in the sound. She stopped abruptly when the restroom door swung wide and two burly men in tan uniforms rushed in. They were followed by a lean, gray-haired man in a gray business suit, who swept us with a cold, all-encompassing glance and said in a deceptively soft voice, "Let the lady up."

"Who're you?" Mike asked.

"This ain't no lady," Mike Hennessy snorted.

"She bites," Danny explained.

"I'm Shevchenko, head of security," the suit said. "Let the lady get up. Now, please."

The two Mikes rose warily and stepped back out of range. Danny, tucking his book under one arm, used the other to help Adele to her feet. Once up, she shook him off.

"I want these men arrested," she demanded. She brushed fussily at her clothing, glaring at Danny. "Particularly that one. He hit me with his big book. Twice."

For a moment we were so stunned by her composure that we simply stood and gaped. Jenny recovered first.

"I don't believe this," she said. "The woman was trying to kill me and she wants him arrested because he hit her with a *book?* She was coming after me with a *knife*, for Christ's sake!"

Shevchenko's eyes narrowed. "A knife?"

"There!" Jenny pointed. "It's right there!"

One of the tan-suited men picked up the knife, holding it by the tip. Shevchenko nodded. He turned to Adele and said politely. "What is your name, ma'am?"

"I'm Mrs. Adele Rountree," Adele stated haughtily. "I'm Mrs. Hamilton Bradford Manville Junior's mother. I'm sure you know who *she* is."

Shevchenko's face remained impassive. "Mrs. Rountree," he said in that quiet voice, "if you will be kind enough to accompany my men to my office, I'm sure we can get this all straightened out."

"I should hope so," Adele sniffed.

When the three had gone, Shevchenko nodded at Danny and Mike Hennessy.

"If you two want to return to your booths, you can go."

"You know us?" Danny asked, surprised.

"The book man. The wife in the wheelchair."

"Sonovagun." Mike Hennessy marvelled. "Shevchenko, I'm impressed. And I don't impress easy."

Shevchenko shrugged. "It's my hotel. You'll be around if we need you?"

"Till nine tonight. And we'll be here all day tomorrow," Danny assured him.

Shevchenko nodded. "And you, Miss Steele," he said, "would you and your friends come with me, please?"

We followed him down a long, empty corridor to a row of glass-enclosed offices. He opened the door to the second cubicle and stood aside for us to enter.

"Mrs. Angelo will order coffee for you," he said. "Or a drink, if you prefer. I'll join you in a few minutes."

Mrs. Angelo was a plump, rather plain young woman with black hair, dark eyes, and a lovely, white smile. She murmured our request for coffee into a phone, produced aspirin and a glass of water for Jenny, an ashtray for Mike, and returned to her computer keyboard.

A white-coated waiter arrived with a large carafe of hot coffee. He set the tray on a filing cabinet and departed. We served ourselves, drinking the coffee gratefully. And waited.

Half an hour passed before Shevchenko reappeared.

"I'm sorry to have kept you waiting," he apologized. "I was unavoidably detained. Please pardon me."

"Sure," Mike said irritably. "Where's Mrs. Rountree?"

"Mrs. Rountree is in my office."

"In your office? What about the police? Haven't you called the police?"

Shevchenko frowned. "Perhaps if Ms. Steele can tell me precisely what happened?"

"I'll tell you *precisely* what happened." Mike butted his cigarette angrily. "Mrs. Rountree followed Ms. Steele to the restroom where she attacked Ms. Steele and Mrs. Wilde with a knife. We stopped her. That is precisely what happened."

Shevchenko looked at me. "You were with Ms. Steele?'

"I was in the restroom before she came. But, yes, I was with her."

"You witnessed the attack?"

"Of course I witnessed the attack. I was there."

"What's going on?" Mike frowned at Shevchenko. "Where are the police? Has Mrs. Rountree been arrested?"

"Mrs. Rountree has called her lawyer. She insists she was the one attacked."

"She . . . you're kidding." Mike's startled eyes darted incredulously from Jenny to me and back to Shevchenko. "She was attacked? What about the knife she had?"

"She says it isn't hers."

Mike's eyes narrowed angrily. "Listen, Shevchenko," he said, enunciating each word with care. "Mrs. Wilde witnessed the entire episode. From start to finish. Three of us, Danny, Mike, and I, saw the knife. We took it from her. That's four witnesses—five, counting Jenny—who know she's lying."

"And I'm sure her lawyer will so advise her," Shevchenko said smoothly. "Meanwhile, I wonder if you'd mind waiting a few minutes longer? The police will need your statements."

"We'll wait," Mike said grimly. "There's no way some hotshot legal flunky is going to talk her out of this one. We'll wait."

"Thank you." Shevchenko nodded politely and left.

A few minutes passed. Then a few more. Jenny closed her eyes, her head tilted back. Mike chain-smoked. The minutes dragged and I found myself nodding. I must have dozed. I snapped back at the sound of Mike's astonished voice.

"Nick! What the hell are you doing here?"

I opened my eyes. Shevchenko had returned. With him was Nick Kramer.

Nick nodded at Mike, glanced at Jenny, and spoke to Shevchenko. "Would you mind? I'd like to talk to these people in private."

"Of course." Shevchenko gestured to Mrs. Angelo. She paused to switch off her computer, then followed him from the room. The door had barely closed when Mike rose angrily to his feet.

"Goddammit, Nick. What's going on? We've been sitting here for over two hours. What the hell is happening? And what the hell are you doing here?"

"Sit down, Mike," Nick said calmly. "And I'll tell you what's happening, all right?" He permitted himself the ghost of a smile. "You're not going to like it, Pop."

"So what else is new?" Mike grumbled, but sat down. "I haven't liked anything about this whole business so far."

Nick circled the desk and sat in Mrs. Angelo's chair. He looked at Jenny. "Are you all right?" he asked gently.

Jenny nodded.

"And you, Catherine?"

"I'm fine, Nick. Thanks." I smiled into those green eyes. "How did you get involved in all this?"

"Rosemary Chang called me."

"Rosemary Chang?" Mike reacted as if he'd been stung. "Don't tell me you're Adele Rountree's lawyer!"

"Relax, Pop. I don't practice criminal law. Rosemary called me because she needed help."

"Okay," Mike conceded. "So what is it I won't like?"

Nick glanced from Mike to me, to Jenny. He spoke directly to her. "The most Adele will ever be charged with is assault with intent to harm."

For a moment there was a stunned silence, then Jenny leaned forward, her face pinched. "What did you say?" she asked.

"What is this, Nick?" Mike was on his feet again. "Some kind of joke? Assault? What about Larry? The woman broke his neck, for God's sake. What about Cody? She stuck a knife in him eight times. I'd call that more than assault with intent to harm. Running Jenny down with her car isn't . . ."

"Pop!" Nick spoke so sharply Mike was silenced. "Listen for a change, okay? Before you bring on another heart attack, just listen, will you?"

Mike glared but sat down. "Okay," he said. "Talk."

"Good." Nick folded his arms across his chest and leaned back in Mrs. Angelo's chair. "I spent an hour with Rosemary, Nancy Lee, and Adele. Then I called Karl Vogel. He and I have been going up and down on it for the last hour. That's why you were kept waiting so long."

"Who's Karl Vogel?" Mike ventured in what was, for him, a timid voice.

"He's a criminal lawyer. One of the best."

"You had to get the best?" Mike snapped, then caved in quickly. "Okay! Okay!"

Nick unfolded his arms. He leaned on the desk and looked at each of us in turn.

"I'm going to talk," he said quietly, "and I don't want to be interrupted. Ethically, I'm way off-base. When I'm finished"—he stared pointedly at Mike—"you can go off the deep end. Not before. Agreed?"

Mike shrugged. "Agreed."

Nick nodded. "First, the marriage certificate. It's valid. Nancy Lee was on a ski vacation in Vermont. She was nineteen at the time. So was Cody. He was a ski instructor. They got married, just for fun, Nancy Lee says. When the vacation was over, she went home and forgot about it."

"Forgot?" Jenny asked incredulously. "She just forgot she was married?"

"If you knew Nancy Lee you wouldn't find that strange," Nick said drily. "It never occurred to her to divorce Cody. Time passed and she became Mrs. Hamilton Bradford Manville Junior. Then, just about a year ago, Cody showed up and demanded money, a lot of money. Nancy Lee told her mother about the marriage, apparently for the first time. Adele told her not to worry. She would meet with Cody. She would talk to Cody."

"*Talk* to Cody?" Mike couldn't resist. "Some talk. She slaughtered the poor bugger."

Nick smiled thinly. "Adele said he made her angry. He wouldn't listen to reason. He deserved to die. He was rude to her."

Unexpectedly, Jenny laughed. "Rude? Poor Jason. He'd have freaked. *Here lies Jason Cody. He was rude.*"

I took Jenny's hand in mine. Hers was cold. Nick eyed her narrowly, then continued.

"She read about Cody's live-in companion the next day and convinced herself Jenny would try to take over where Cody left off. She assumed she'd eliminated Jenny when she ran her down. Then Jenny reappeared, very much alive."

For a moment there was silence. I tried to imagine Adele's state of mind upon hearing Jenny's distinctive voice again, a voice she thought she had silenced.

"So she tried again," Nick continued, "and the wrong harlequin died. By then she was in an emotional frenzy. She had to keep on killing Jenny. And Jenny wouldn't die."

"Are you saying she's crazy?" Mike frowned.

"No." Nick shook his head. "She's not insane."

"Not insane?" Mike's brows lifted. "Killing twice, attacking Jenny three times, this is sane?"

"People kill for any number of reasons. Their reasoning may be skewed, but they're not necessarily insane." Nick looked at Jenny. "Adele was convinced you were a threat. A threat she had to eliminate."

"I didn't even know them." Jenny's shoulders lifted. "Who was I a threat to? Nancy Lee?"

"Depends on who you talk to," Nick said.

"What does that mean?" I asked.

Nick's green eyes smiled at me. "If you talk to Adele, Jenny is a fiend, intent on ruining Nancy Lee's life. She, Adele, is a mother bear, fiercely protecting her child. She maintains she had every right. It's a law of nature."

"Hoo boy," Mike grunted. "And you say she's sane?"

"If you talk to Nancy Lee," Nick continued, "Adele was fiercely protecting her own socially prestigious connection with the Manvilles."

"What do you think?" I asked.

Nick shrugged. "Either. Both."

"Do you think Nancy Lee knew what her mother was doing?" I asked. "Killing people left and right?"

Nick shook his head. "It's hard to say. Nancy Lee denies knowing about, or having any complicity in, the murders her mother committed."

"Do you believe her?" I asked. "Do you believe she really didn't know what her mother was doing?"

"It doesn't matter what I believe. Adele claims Nancy Lee collaborated. Nancy Lee claims she didn't. She says she couldn't have cared less what Cody did. Being Mrs. Hamilton Bradford Manville was getting to be a crashing bore. And she never liked Ham much anyway."

"What about Rosemary Chang? What did she have to say?"

"Rosemary? Rosemary had one word to say. 'Typical.'"

"That's *all*? She's just found out her mother, and maybe her sister, are murderers and all she has to say is *typical*?" I was nonplused. "These are very strange people."

Nick's eyes were mildly amused. "Like the man said, the rich, they are different."

Mike waited a moment to ensure Nick had finished, then said, "What I don't get is, how come the only crime Adele will be charged with is assault?"

"Think about it. Jason Cody. On the strength of a marriage license alone, which is all there is, she probably wouldn't even be indicted. And if she were to be, any good defense lawyer would tear the case to shreds. There's nothing concrete to link her to Cody. No fingerprints were found on the knife she used to kill Cody. It was November. Adele wore gloves and she says she never took them off. Even the building itself no longer exists."

"What about Jenny? Does Adele have a red car?"

"She did then. She doesn't now. It could be traced, but there's no way of proving, after almost a year, that it was the car used to run Jenny down."

"What about Larry's car?" Mike brightened. "I don't recall Adele wearing gloves with her costume. Wouldn't there be fingerprints, or something, on the trunk lid?"

"I called Nathan Lewison, Larry's lawyer. The car was sold to a dealer as soon as the police released it, early this week. I checked with the dealer. The car was washed and waxed and sold immediately. The police are convinced Larry was killed by a mugger. Without a witness to place Adele in the parking lot at the time . . ." Nick shrugged.

"What about you?" I asked. "If Adele told you she killed them, couldn't you . . . what . . . testify? Or something?"

Nick's face closed down. "No. Rosemary is no fool. Before she would let Adele talk to me, she hired me to act as counsel. I could be disbarred for what I've told you."

We were silent as each of us, separately, comprehended the trust Nick had placed in us. Finally, Jenny, in a small voice said, "So there's only the assault?"

Nick looked at her and his face softened. "I think you better take a look at that too, Jenny."

"What do you mean?"

"Karl assured me if you press charges he'll mess up your life for the next few years. He'll use every trick he knows. Delays, postponements, whatever. He'll drag you back here to appear over and over again. Not only you. Mike, Catherine, Danny, and the Hennessys. And Rafe and Charlie. He'll plead temporary insanity. He'll plead menopause, sunspots, moon madness, and the effect of insecticides on broccoli. Whatever it takes. By the time Karl's through, the whole thing will read like a minor assault and she'll get off with a slap on the wrist. In the meanwhile, it'll have cost all of you a lot of time and money."

"Is he aware she killed Jason and Larry?" Jenny asked.

"That's irrelevant," Nick said tersely. "He is only concerned with the assault charge."

"Is all that moon madness stuff legal? Can he actually do what he says?"

"He can. And as long as Adele has the money to pay him, you can be sure he will."

Mike shook his head in disbelief. "As long as Adele has the money. Two murders? And, as long as she has the money to pay some hotshot lawyer, the most she'll probably suffer is inconvenience. This is justice?"

"Welcome to the real world," Nick said quietly.

"The real world stinks," Jenny said sourly. She looked at me, then at Nick. "What do you think I should do?"

"That's up to you," Nick said. "How important is it to you to see Adele arrested?"

"Arrested?"

"If you lay charges, she'll be arrested."

"She'll go to jail?"

"Jail?" Nick gave her a half-smile. "Not today. She'll be arrested, taken to the local precinct, and charged. Karl will bail her out immediately and she'll go home."

"Will they handcuff her?"

"I doubt it."

"What? No handcuffs?" Jenny snapped. "Well, what the hell, that's no fun."

"Forget fun," Nick said sharply. "Believe me, none of this will be fun. I think you'd better think seriously about it right now. In terms of your career. Right now, you're hot. Is having Adele arrested worth complicating your life at this point in time?"

Jenny studied him with narrowed eyes. Then her mouth thinned. She drew a deep breath and released it.

"Screw the career," she said. "Jason may have been a waste of space but he didn't deserve to die. Not the way he did. And Larry . . . Aw, Larry . . ." Her eyes misted suddenly. A single tear spilled over.

She brushed at her cheek with her fingertips and glared at Nick.

"Okay." The word came out flat and hard. "Go tell your shyster friend I'm pressing charges. And tell that wacko client of his she's going to be busted, courtesy of me."

"You're sure?" Nick asked. He rose from behind the desk.

"I'm sure." Jenny's nose wrinkled ruefully. "Right at this moment anyway. So you better go do it fast."

"Hold it a second." Mike raised his hand in a traffic cop's gesture. He let it drop and leaned forward. "Nick? How long for this thing to get to trial?"

Nick shrugged. "By the time we go through the prelims? It could take a year. Two? Maybe longer."

"This lawyer of hers . . . I've forgotten his name."

"Vogel," Nick prompted, "Karl Vogel."

"Right." Mike nodded. "Karl Vogel. You said he was the best criminal lawyer in town?"

"One of the best."

"Which means, I assume, he doesn't come cheap?"

"No." Nick shook his head, smiling. "Karl Vogel does not come cheap. And every minute we sit here chatting is costing Adele money."

"What if she runs out of money?"

Nick's eyes narrowed. "Is that likely?"

"It could happen. According to Kitty Drummond, Adele is broke. Not our kind of broke. But she has had to make do without the little niceties like a chauffeur, a gardener, and an upstairs maid. Would you say a lawyer of Karl Vogel's caliber will put a dent in her budget?"

"A very substantial dent," Nick agreed, amused.

"So, if Jenny presses charges, Adele will be paying a very expensive lawyer a lot of money for quite a while."

"That's how it works."

"A couple of years of a high-priced lawyer like Vogel could even bankrupt her?"

Nick's shoulders lifted in the merest hint of a shrug. "It wouldn't be the first time it's happened."

"Good," Mike grunted. "Let's hope Vogel meant what he said about his delay-and-postponement strategy. He'll be making endless court appearances and it'll all go on Adele's tab." He frowned up at Nick. "Which precinct will they take her to? The fifth?"

"I imagine so. Why?"

"I'm going to call Kitty Drummond. Let her know who is being arrested and why and where. See if she can arrange to have maybe a reporter and a photographer waiting for Adele. *Prominent Socialite Arrested for Attempted Murder.*"

"Assault," Nick corrected.

"Arrested is all it needs. And when Kitty drops a few more words—like murder and bigamy—in a few malicious ears Adele might as well take herself off to a leper colony. If she can find one. The Manville crowd will cut her dead."

"The unkindest cut of all," Nick murmured. He looked at Jenny. "When do you go back to New York?"

"Tonight."

"I'd like to drive you to the airport," Nick said. "If you like, we can have dinner first. All of us, of course," he added.

Mike and I pleaded senility and exhaustion.

"You won't mind if I go with Nick?" Jenny asked.

"Good, Lord, no. Go. Enjoy."

Nick circled the desk. He took Jenny's arm. "Okay, let's do it," he said. "I'll give Karl your decision and we can get out of here."

Mike picked up the phone. I followed Jenny and Nick to the last office in the corridor. It was identical to the one we had just left.

Through the glass we could see Rosemary, bulky and shapeless in a badly creased gray linen suit, leaning against the window frame, her head turned away from her sister and mother, her gaze fixed outside. Nancy Lee sat on the corner of the desk, one foot swinging languidly, her extraordinary eyes fixed on her pale kid sandal, her exquisite face serene, as detached from what was happening in that small room as if she was alone among strangers.

Adele was seated in an office chair, back erect, hair unkempt, mouth thinned to a lipless line, her hands gripping the large handbag in her lap.

A very short, balding man stood in front of her, well into her space. His eyes, the same golden hazel as Charlie's, were magnified behind thick, dark-rimmed glasses. The collar of his blue striped shirt was unbuttoned, his tie loosened. He stabbed the air inches from Adele's face with a stubby forefinger, talking vehemently.

"That's Karl Vogel?" Jenny asked.

"That's Karl Vogel," Nick replied. He tapped lightly on the door and entered immediately. Four heads swivelled as he stepped into the room.

His back was to us. We could neither see his expression nor hear what he said. But there was no mistaking the moment when he delivered the bottom line. Adele's face contorted and she lunged from her chair.

Karl Vogel, with more strength than I would have thought such a small man could summon, pushed her back down, his palms flat against her chest.

She hit the chair with a spine-jarring thud. She glared up at Karl, past him toward Nick, and caught sight of Jenny beyond the glass partition.

Sheer hatred flashed across her face, an expression so malevolent that I felt my scalp prickle. I glanced at Jenny fearfully.

Jenny was staring as intently as though Adele was an exotic specimen under glass. Her eyes locked with Adele's, held for an icy second, then she turned and walked away.

She reached the cross-corridor terminating the hallway and leaned against the wall, her arms folded across her breasts, her head bent low.

I followed her.

"Jenny?" All I could see was the clean, white part on the top of her head. I reached out and gently stroked the fall of glossy hair obscuring her face. "Are you all right?"

She raised her head. Her eyes were an electric blue.

"Did you see the way she looked at me?" Her voice was husky, intense. "Did you see her face when she saw me?"

She raised her arms, raked her fingers through her hair, and pulled it tightly back from her face.

"Her eyes! Did you see the venom in those eyes? My God, that was pure, unadulterated murder. Nobody's ever looked at me like that before."

"I know, I know," I soothed. "But there's nothing she can do to you now. Don't let her frighten you."

Jenny raised startled brows at me. She dropped her arms, letting her hair fall.

"Frighten me?" she said. "She doesn't frighten me. But I sure would like to know how she did it." She poked her cheek with a forefinger. "Which facial muscles does a person use to produce an expression like that?"

I gazed at her in astonishment as her lips thinned to a pink slash above her chin. The skin on her cheeks tightened, her nostrils whitened. She glared at me.

"More in the eyes, I think," I said weakly.

The eyelids narrowed, hooded over darkening irises. It was probably a trick of light, but her large, nearsighted pupils seemed to shrink to pinpoints. In spite of myself, I felt a twinge of atavistic alarm.

"Is that it?" she growled.

"Oh God, yes. Only worse."

Her face relaxed. "Worse?" she said. "Really?"

"Really." I drew a deep breath. "I mean, *really*."

"Fantastic." She laughed exultantly. "So, thank you Adele, you pathetic old bag, and up yours."

She raised a defiant middle finger and gestured down the hall just as Mike and Shevchenko emerged from the first office we had occupied. They came to a halt in front of the second office door and Mike said something that brought a laugh from Shevchenko.

Shevchenko opened the door and disappeared into the office. Mike came to join us, grinning to himself.

"What?" I asked him.

"What do you mean *what*?"

"The big smile. And stone-face Shevchenko laughs. What did you say to him?"

"I asked him if he was related to Taras."

"What?"

"It's a Ukie thing, Cat. Taras Shevchenko was a great Ukrainian poet. I asked him if he was related."

"And is he?"

"Of course. He said every Shevchenko he's ever met on three continents is related to Taras. Said he wondered when the old boy found time to write his poetry."

"Oh. Ha. So what did Kitty Drummond have to say?"

Mike's smile broadened.

"She loves it," he gloated. "Asked me if I'd like TV cameras, too. She's calling all her press club cronies and arranging a proper reception committee at the fifth precinct. She said it was a quiet news week and the media'd be all over Adele's story like flies on doggy doo."

Jenny clapped her hands together gleefully. "Yay, Mike," she crowed. "More fun, more people killed!"

"What?"

She grinned at me. "It's a line from one of the *Halls of Justice* scripts. We all sort of adopted it. More fun, more people killed? It means . . . uh . . ." She glanced past me. "I guess you had to be there. Here comes Nick."

Nick came down the hallway toward us. Without breaking stride he pressed us around the cross-corridor corner, out of sight of the office row.

"All set," he said. "Shevchenko is calling the police. We can leave now."

"I don't have to be here?" Jenny asked.

"No." Nick took Jenny's arm. "Let's go."

"Just a minute." Jenny stepped away from Nick and kissed Mike's cheek. "Thanks, Mike. You're an old sweetie pie."

"Yeah. I know. You take care, kid."

She turned to me. "I have a free weekend between New York and L.A., Cat," she said shyly. "Can I come home?"

"Of course you can come home. Anytime."

"Thank you." She put her arms around me and pressed her cheek to mine. "Thank you for everything," she said softly.

I felt a rush of affection for her. For this Jenny.

Whatever happened to Jennifer Steele—fame, stardom, mediocrity, obscurity, whatever—she would never be this Jenny again. I hugged her, hard, then we stepped apart.

We watched them walk away from us, Mike and I, Nick with his arm circling Jenny's shoulders, Jenny with her arm about his waist, laughingly matching his stride.

"Look at them," I said. "Two young, beautiful people. What's going to happen to them, Mike? What's the world going to do to them?"

"Probably the same thing it does to everybody. Kick 'em in the crotch." Mike linked his arm through mine. "Don't worry, Cat. They'll survive."

We turned and went back down the hallway, to the antique show, to tell Charlie and Rafe and Danny and Mike and Ros Hennessy the end of the story.